Little A.J. turned his gapped-tooth smile on Brooke. He offered the banana.

Brooke exchanged smiles with Gabe. "Someone is raising him right."

"I'm doing my best. I'm a widower," Gabe said.

"I'm sorry. That must be really hard."

"Child care's not easy to find in Clayton."

Brooke stilled, her expression part yearning and part fear, neither of which Gabe understood.

"Would you be interested in the nanny job?"

Her eyes widened. "I...can't."

She'd dismissed his offer, yet her gaze followed every move A.J. made. A.J. high-stepped into Brooke's legs and wrapped his arms around her knees, gurgled something and grinned up at her.

What was that look in Brooke's pretty eyes?

* * *

Rocky Mountain Heirs:
When the greatest fortune of all is love.

The Nanny's Homecoming—Linda Goodnight
July 2011

The Sheriff's Runaway Bride—Arlene James
August 2011

The Doctor's Family—Lenora Worth
September 2011

The Cowboy's Lady—Carolyne Aarsen
October 2011

The Loner's Thanksgiving Wish—Roxanne Rustand
November 2011

The Prodigal's Christmas Reunion—Kathryn Springer
December 2011

Books by Linda Goodnight

Love Inspired

In the Spirit of...Christmas
A Very Special Delivery
*A Season for Grace
*A Touch of Grace
*The Heart of Grace
Missionary Daddy
A Time to Heal
Home to Crossroads Ranch
The Baby Bond
**Finding Her Way Home
**The Wedding Garden
The Lawman's Christmas Wish
**A Place to Belong
The Nanny's Homecoming

*The Brothers' Bond
**Redemption River

LINDA GOODNIGHT

Winner of a RITA® Award for excellence in inspirational fiction, Linda Goodnight has also won a Booksellers' Best, ACFW Book of the Year and a Reviewers' Choice Award from *RT Book Reviews*. Linda has appeared on the Christian bestseller list and her romance novels have been translated into more than a dozen languages. Active in orphan ministry, this former nurse and teacher enjoys writing fiction that carries a message of hope and light in a sometimes dark world. She and her husband, Gene, live in Oklahoma. Readers can write to her at linda@lindagoodnight.com, or c/o Love Inspired Books, 233 Broadway, Suite 1001, New York, NY 10279.

The Nanny's Homecoming

Linda Goodnight

Love Inspired

Special thanks and acknowledgment to
Linda Goodnight for her contribution
to the Rocky Mountain Heirs miniseries.

Recycling programs
for this product may
not exist in your area.

™ LOVE INSPIRED BOOKS

ISBN-13: 978-0-373-81558-6

THE NANNY'S HOMECOMING

Copyright © 2011 by Harlequin Books S.A.

www.LoveInspiredBooks.com

Printed in U.S.A.

A man's heart devises his way:
but the Lord directs his steps.
—*Proverbs* 16:9

For family, friends, and most of all
for my Lord Jesus, "in whom I live and move and
have my being." I could not do this without You.

Prologue

George Clayton Sr. did three things before he died. He made his peace with God. He sold the Lucky Lady Silver Mine to a fella out of Denver named Gabe Wesson. And he wrote a will.

Now, it was the will that brought the simmering pot of Clayton, Colorado, to a full-out, rolling boil. The way old George figured it, sometimes a wound's got to fester before it can heal.

And fester it did.

Chapter One

Gabe Wesson was a desperate man.

Inside the aptly named Cowboy Café, a hodge-podge of western types and various other towns-folk gathered at the long, Formica-topped counter for homemade pie and socializing. Gabe joined the counter crowd, his toddler son perched on his knee.

In a few short weeks, he'd discovered that if a man wanted to know anything or spread any news in the town of Clayton, Colorado, the Cowboy Café was the place to do it. Today, what he needed more than anything was a nanny for his son, A.J. Funny that he could run a corporation with dozens of employees but he'd hit a brick wall when it came to finding suitable child care in this tiny Rocky Mountain town.

He was a gambler of sorts, a speculator. Some

would even call him a troublemaker, though he always left a place better than he'd found it.

He'd found Clayton to be a sleepy community time had forgotten. With an abandoned railroad track slicing through town and an equally abandoned silver mine perched in the nearby hills, the town was just about dead.

It was the "just about" that had brought Gabe here. He had a knack for sniffing out near-dead businesses and bringing them back to life. This gift—and he was convinced it was a gift from God—had taken him from a scrappy kid stocking groceries to the head of his own Denver corporation by the age of thirty-three.

But unless he found a nanny soon, he would be forced to move back to Denver, something he did not want to do. At least not now, not when the weight of the past two years was starting to lift.

The friendly young waitress, Kylie Jones, sailed past with a slice of hot pie oozing cherries and drowning in vanilla ice cream. Gabe's mouth watered. He ordered the pie and a coffee for himself and a grilled cheese with milk for his son.

Filled with the smell of home-baked cakes and cinnamon, the long, narrow café was warm, welcoming and always busy. Square wooden tables with chunky, straight-backed chairs crowded every space. The *Denver Post,* well-read and refolded, lay next to the old-fashioned cash register and a credit card machine. From a jukebox beside the door, George Strait sang about the best day of his life.

On the stool next to Gabe a cowboy type in boots and Wranglers angled a fork toward the street. A white hearse crept past. "They're planting old George today."

"Cody Jameson, show some respect." Red-haired Erin Fields, the surprisingly young café owner, took a swipe at the worn counter with her bleach rag. "This town wouldn't exist without George Clayton and his family."

Kylie, carefully filling a salt shaker, looked up. "Nobody liked him that much, Erin, even if he was the only lawyer in town. Or maybe because of it."

"Still. Speaking ill of the dead doesn't seem right. His grandkids are here for the funeral and *they're* good people." She propped a hand on one hip and gazed at the street. "Brooke came in yesterday and bought burgers to take over to Arabella's. That girl is still sweet as that cherry pie."

"I'd love to see Brooke again," Kylie said wistfully. She'd moved on to stuffing paper napkins into tall, metal holders. "We played basketball together in high school. She was a terrific point guard."

Erin tossed the bleach rag into the sink behind

the counter and ran her hands under the faucet. "Then see her, Kylie. None of the Clayton kids have been in town for ages, but she'll probably stick around for a couple of days."

Kylie's pretty face tightened. "You know how Vincent feels about that side of his family."

Erin's lips thinned but she didn't say anymore. She took a pair of roast-beef-laden platters from the order window, grabbed an iced tea pitcher and moved toward a couple seated at one of the square tables.

Gabe listened with interest, gleaning the facts and the undercurrents. He'd returned to Clayton this morning after a three-day trip to corporate headquarters in Denver. Between then and now, the former owner of the Lucky Lady Silver Mine, George Clayton, had passed away. He wondered if George's heirs knew he'd sold the mine to an outsider.

While he contemplated what the unexpected death could mean to his company, Kylie stopped in front of A.J. A trim brunette, she was the fiancée of one of his new employees, Vincent Clayton. She always made a fuss over A.J.

"What a big boy you are. You ate up every bite of that sandwich." She felt A.J.'s muscles and received a giggle in return.

Fork paused at half-mast, Gabe said, "My job offer is still open."

"Sorry, no. I'd love to nanny A.J., but I'm getting married soon."

Gabe didn't know what getting married had to do with his offer, but he let the comment pass. "Got any other ideas for me? I need to find someone soon." Like yesterday.

Her brown ponytail swung side to side. "I've been asking everyone who comes in. So has Erin, and your sign is still up." She pointed to the fancy graphic-enhanced poster stuck to the front door. "So far, no luck. Who's looking after him now?"

"Me, mostly." That's what made the situation desperate. A job site, especially a construction zone, was no place for a curious toddler. Gabe sweated bullets every time he had to go to the mine. As work progressed, he'd need to be there more and more.

"Let me know if you hear anything, okay?" He took out his wallet and tossed a bill on the counter. "Keep the change."

Kylie's eyes widened at the size of the bill. "Wow, thank you, Mr. Wesson. I'll keep asking."

With a nod toward the cowboy and a wave toward the redhead, Gabe and A.J. pushed out into the summer sun as the last of the funeral cars crawled by. A pretty woman with wavy blond hair gazed bleakly through the passenger window. Something in her expression touched a chord in him. He knew he was staring but couldn't seem to help himself. A.J., tired of standing still, yanked at his father's hand. The woman, stirred by the motion, looked up. Their eyes met and held. Sensation prickled Gabe's skin.

The car rolled on past and she was gone. But the vision of those sad blue eyes stayed behind.

Brooke Clayton gazed around at the collection of Clayton grandchildren gathered in the conference room of the Clayton Christian Church like a bunch of errant schoolchildren sent to the principal's office. Not one of them wanted to be here at the reading of their grandfather's will. Yet, five of the six had come out of blood loyalty, not for Grandpa George Clayton, but for their cousin Arabella. It was her phone call, her need, that had brought them together again after more than four years.

Brooke's gaze rested on each beloved face. Her intense cop brother, Zach. Her sophisticated sister, Vivienne. Mei, the adopted sister of the only absent grandchild, rebel Lucas, and of course, darkly pretty Arabella. With a clutch of emotion, Brooke acknowledged she'd missed them, though she hadn't missed the painful memories of living in the tiny town that bore her family name.

Only family and a few close friends had attended Grandpa George's funeral services, although plenty of townspeople had stared at the procession on its journey to the cemetery. She wondered what they were thinking. Good riddance? Was there anyone who'd miss George Clayton, Sr.? None of the grandchildren had it in them to pretend what they didn't feel, and silly as it sounded, the lack of grief had made Brooke sad.

As they'd driven down Railroad Street, a man had stepped out of the Cowboy Café. A tall, handsome stranger with a very small boy.

That's when she'd begun to weep. Small children had that effect on her.

She'd once known everyone in this town of less than a thousand, but she hadn't recognized the man. They'd made eye contact, and something— some indefinable something—had passed between them. She'd thought about him and his beautiful brown-haired son off and on during the graveside service. Who was he? Why had that particular stranger's image been stamped on her memory?

"We need to begin." Pencil thin in an appropriately black suit, attorney Mark Arrington had already waited more than an hour for the sixth and final grandchild to arrive.

Calls had been made and letters sent, but no one was certain their rebellious cousin had received the summons. Even if he had, only one person in the room was confident of Lucas's attendance. His sister.

Brooke wiggled her feet inside the confining

heels. With a broken pinky, pinching heels and her wounded pride, she hurt everywhere. A few days ago, she was planning a wedding. Now, she had no plans at all beyond getting through today.

"I don't think Lucas is going to make it," she said.

"If Lucas was coming, he'd be here," Zach added with coplike frankness.

"A few minutes longer." The quiet steel of Mei Clayton's voice drew every eye to her round, delicate face. Of all her kin, Brooke understood Mei the least. As she'd grown older Mei had pulled away from all of the Claytons except her adopted brother, Lucas.

"What makes you think he'll show?" Zach asked.

Mei sat up straighter in the cushioned chair, quietly insistent. Her gleaming black hair swung softly around her Asian features. "If he's needed, my brother will come."

The lawyer cleared his throat. "I'm sorry, everyone. I have another appointment in thirty minutes." With a gesture Brooke found overdramatic, the attorney pointed toward a flat screen. "If I may direct your attention to the TV. Mr. Clayton himself would like to address you first, and then I have the task of setting out the rules of the will."

Brooke exchanged frowning glances with her brother. What in the world? Zach lifted an eyebrow but offered no response. Whatever his thoughts, he'd keep them to himself until all the evidence was on the table.

The screen flickered to life and the face of Grandpa George appeared, looking a little too hearty to have been buried a few hours ago. Dressed in his usual dark business suit, he was seated behind the desk at his law offices. An uncomfortable hush fell over the five assembled Claytons.

"If you're watching this, I'm dead." George chuckled at his own morbid joke. *"You're all wondering why I've dragged you back here. I haven't been the best grandfather. I haven't always done right by you, or by anyone, for that matter. But before the deaths of my two sons changed everything, we were a family. Not as close as we should have been, but we spent Christmas and Thanksgiving together."*

"Then because of issues I hope you never know about, I lost my daughter, too. Kat won't even speak to me, and five of you grandkids have scattered across the country. Clayton, Colorado, might not be much, but it's your home, your history. My daddy started this town. My wife started the church. Claytons belong here." He pointed a bony finger toward the camera. *"You belong here."*

The cousins exchanged uncomfortable glances.

Brooke knew they were all thinking the same thing. Having a dead man point at you was weird.

"I want you to come home," Grandpa said. *"All six of you—for at least a year. Be a family again. Revive this dying town. Find your hearts and souls right here where you left them."*

Zach pushed up from his chair and paced to the window.

"Sit down, Zach. You always did pace like a tiger when upset." Grandpa George chuckled. *"If you didn't get up, you wanted to."*

Zach returned his attention the video, arms folded, mouth quirked in wry amusement. Goose bumps shimmied up Brooke's back. Zach's philosophy might be "Never let 'em see you sweat," but Brooke was all for sweating. Grandpa George's video bordered on creepy.

"You may think Clayton is your past, son," Grandpa George went on. *"But I know a thing or two about your present. Miami holds nothing but bad memories for you. Clayton and this county need you. Even dead, your old grandpa can pull a few strings, and you'd do mighty fine as Clayton County sheriff. Think about it, Zach."*

Zach as county sheriff? Now there was an outrageously interesting and laughable idea. After what Zach had been through in Clayton? No way.

"As incentive, because I know none of you will willingly come home, I've left something for each

of you." Grandpa George paused. Brooke refused to even ponder an inheritance. The old miser had probably left them all a pile of debts just for orneriness. *"Two hundred fifty thousand dollars each, plus five hundred acres of Colorado real estate right here in Clayton County."*

A clamor broke out in the room.

"How could he have had that much money?"

"I thought he was broke."

"I can't believe this."

Mark Arrington lifted a long hand. "Ladies. Zach. There are stipulations to the inheritance. You need to hear the rest."

Vivienne rolled her thickly lashed blue eyes. "Stipulations. That figures."

The clamor subsided, but Brooke's heart clattered wildly in her chest until she could barely hear her grandfather's voice. A quarter of a million dollars? She could…she could do anything she wanted to. If she knew what that was.

"Arabella."

Her cousin jumped. How many times in the past months had kind-hearted Arabella jumped up to do their sick grandfather's bidding?

"You're the only one who's stuck with your old Grandpa. That's why I'm leaving you the house, too, as long as your cousins cooperate and stick out their year. Without you, I wouldn't have made my peace with God. Leastways, Reverend West

says the Lord forgives my sins, and though that doesn't make up for the wrongs I've done, perhaps this legacy of good I'm leaving behind will make a difference."

Arabella dabbed at her eyes. She'd worried a tissue into a ragged mess. Mei reached into her handbag and pulled out a handful of tissues, offering them to her cousin without a word.

"So there you are, children," Grandpa George said. *"An inheritance that can change your lives if you choose to accept it. But the will is ironclad. No exceptions. All of you have to spend a year in Clayton. And you have to come home by this Christmas. Hear that, Lucas?"* He rapped twice on the desk. *"No later than Christmas.*

"This is my chance to leave a legacy—a good one—for the town that bears my name. I know what you're thinking—too little, too late—but I ask that each of you look in your hearts and find one happy memory of me. It might take a while, and you might be reluctant, but you'll find at least one. And maybe it'll help."

The television screen flickered and went dark. The conference room was so quiet Brooke could hear her finger throb.

Mark Arrington cleared his throat. "So there you have it. Spend one year in Clayton and inherit a fortune."

Vivienne, elegant and classy in black and white,

was already shaking her dark blond head. As a renowned New York chef, she had worked hard to shed her rural ways. She loved the city. She loved her life. "I can't just walk away from my career. What am I supposed to do in Clayton? Flip burgers at The Cowboy Café?"

"We all have jobs, Viv," Zach said quietly.

Well, that wasn't exactly true. But Brooke was too embarrassed to bring up her homeless, jobless state at a time like this. Both her siblings had great careers. Important jobs that mattered. Brooke had never wanted to come back to Clayton, but now... The others had lives. She didn't. An inheritance of this caliber could change everything.

"If we do this, we all have to agree," she said. "A quarter of a million dollars is a lot of money for any of us. Even you, Vivienne."

Zach, who was up pacing again, spun around. "You're forgetting something—or *someone*. Lucas. Does anyone even know where he is? Anyone talked to him lately?"

They all looked to Mei who sat apart, serene and alone. Long black hair swished across her slender shoulders as she shook her head. "Not in weeks."

Vivienne blew out an exasperated breath. Like Brooke, she bore the Clayton looks—their father's looks. Blond, blue-eyed, a single dimple in her left cheek. Unlike the others, she'd studied at Le

Cordon Bleu in Paris and had an air of sophistication totally out of place in Clayton, Colorado. "We could spend a year in Clayton for nothing."

"I say we forget about it," Mei said. "None of us wants to be here. The chance of actually inheriting anything but trouble is slim at best. I don't want to waste a year of my life in this town for nothing."

Nods of agreement circled the room. Mei had spoken for them all.

"If I may say something please." The lawyer took a manila folder from the table in front of him. "No one has asked what will happen to the money should the six of you fail to inherit."

Zach shoved an agitated hand over his military-style haircut. "What happens?"

Mark opened the folder. "This is in your grandfather's handwriting, notarized and witnessed as part of his last will and testament. He says, *'Should any of you choose not to spent one full year in Clayton, the entire inheritance, including the family home, with apologies to my dear Arabella, will go to Samuel Clayton. We've had our share of bad history, but he is my brother.'*"

"What? That's crazy." Vivienne's blue eyes flashed. "There's no way Grandpa would leave anything to Great-Uncle Samuel or his clan of rotten Claytons."

Mark offered the folder for Vivienne's perusal. "I tend to agree with your sentiment, Vivienne, but your grandfather was adamant. After his spiritual awakening, he felt badly about some of the things he'd done to his brother."

They all knew the story. Grandpa George had not only stolen Samuel's girl and married her, but he'd also convinced his ailing, blind father, Great-Grandpa Isaac, that, as an attorney, he was best suited to handle the family landholdings. Grandpa George had wound up owning most of Clayton, whereas Samuel had only his home and a few acres. The resulting bad blood had flowed into Samuel's three sons and their children, too.

"Some of us have too many wounds from Great-Uncle Samuel and his bunch to let them inherit anything," Brooke said as she stroked Zach's shoulder. The muscles beneath her hand were rock hard with tension. She remembered the lies Vincent Clayton had told that had almost destroyed Zach's dream.

"There are some decent people in this town," Mei said. "We all know what Great-Uncle Samuel's bunch would do with that kind of power and money."

Grimly, Vivienne nodded. "Destroy everything in their rotten path. I don't know if I can take off a year, but—"

Mei's melodic voice finished the thought. "We have to try."

Zach stretched a hand toward them, palm down, the way they'd done as kids. "Agreed?"

Like old times. One for all. All for one.

"Agreed." Brooke slapped her hand over her brother's and looked to the others.

Slowly, one at a time, with doubt and uncertainty hovering, the other three joined the circle of family and added a hand to the tentative promise.

They would try.

But it was the missing hand that had them all worried. What if Lucas didn't come?

Chapter Two

The summer morning was cool, as still and fresh-smelling as only mountain air can be, and the sun streaked pale gold through fat white clouds. Brooke, breath coming in small puffs, jogged down the hillside and around the curvy road of Bluebird Lane leading to the white frame home where she, Zach and Vivienne had come of age. The old place looked weary and sagged a little but Arabella, the eternal optimist, had done her best to keep the house livable.

After a short trip to Colorado Springs to pack and give up her apartment, Brooke had arrived late last night, three days after the reading of the will, still in a quandary. She was here, in the near ghost town of Clayton, beginning a year that might lead to nowhere. Unless her siblings and cousins followed through—a prospect that worried her a lot—she'd be no better off in a year than she was now.

She'd called her former fiancé and apologized. She was still embarrassed about the fit she'd thrown that day in his car—a door-slamming fit that had broken her pinky finger. A part of her had been hoping he'd changed his mind, that the wedding she'd been meticulously planning was back on. Marty had been polite but firm and cool. In the days since their breakup, his time in prayer had brought him to one conclusion. He and Brooke were a comfortable habit—not a match made in heaven.

He'd mentioned nothing about the original reason for the breakup. Nothing about the disagreement over having children. He was leaving next week, he'd said, for a year of mission's work in Guatemala.

In three days, the man with whom she'd planned to spend her life had moved on without her.

Running shoes slapped the gravel road as she pushed harder. Marty's words had stung. The reminder that she'd once prayed about everything also stung.

Somewhere in the last exciting year of finishing college, making wedding plans with Marty and dreaming of distant lands and needy souls, God had grown further and further away.

Now she wondered if God had intentionally pushed her out, because she'd make a lousy missionary's wife—she couldn't even speak Spanish—and she was too unreliable to take care of His children. Anyone's children.

Her eyes, protected by sunglasses slick with sweat, cut toward the creek that ran behind her family home. If she listened closely, she could hear the pretty, happy sound of clear, cold water trickling over rocks. Water could be so deceptive.

And men, even Christian men, could be so cruel. Marty hadn't understood her fear of having children. He'd said he did at first, but he never really had.

She tugged her attention toward more comfortable thoughts. Someone, she noted with interest, had bought the house next door. The luxury home had been empty for a while—ever since the local doctor passed away and his wife had moved to Oklahoma to live near her daughter. Now the closest medical care was miles away.

Home buyers in Clayton, Colorado, were as rare as medical care. On the day of the funeral, she'd heard mention that the old Lucky Lady Mine might be opened again and that some hotshot front man from Denver had moved to town. Could he be the new neighbor? Someone with a corporate job would be the only person who could afford the doctor's home.

By now she'd reached her long, covered front

porch. Hot, thirsty and eager for a shower, she reached beneath a flowerpot for the key. It was gone.

Weird. The key had been there when she'd left. She was certain. She'd put it there herself. Although most people in Clayton rarely locked their doors, she'd been living in Colorado Springs for the past four years. She always locked up, and as she and her family had done her entire life, she'd stuck the extra key beneath the flowerpot. She tilted each of the other pots. Nothing.

Puzzled, she rattled the doorknob for good measure, then jogged around to the back.

As she'd known it would be, the back door was locked, too.

By now, she was frustrated and a little nervous. She was sure she'd put the key under the pot. Her family had *always* kept the key there. Vivienne and Zach each had a key, but they'd gone back to their respective cities of New York and Miami. They'd both agreed to return, but Brooke wasn't sure about her siblings. They had jobs, lives, futures right where they were.

Brooke had a locked door, a missing key and a case of nervous worry. Someone must have taken her key.

No, that was silly. Why would anyone steal the key without going inside the house?

Her eyes cut to the curtained window. She hoped no one had gone inside.

After one final, frustrated rattle of the knob, she eyed the side of the house and her bedroom window. With an exasperated sigh, she turned in that direction.

Gabe leaned against a fluted column at the corner of his newly acquired back porch with his morning coffee and spoke into his cell phone. "Not everyone's happy about reopening the mine."

On the other end of the line, his lawyer and best friend, Manny Ortega, replied. "People don't like change."

Gabe understood that. His own life had changed often and much, and sometimes change hurt so badly it cut you in half. He'd been there. Tara's death had taken a lot out of him. Being here in Clayton was the kind of change he needed to get him on track again. The slower pace gave him more time to pray and refuel.

"I hired a local, Vincent Clayton, to round up potential labor and smooth ruffled feathers."

"One of *the* Claytons?"

"Oh, yeah. He let me know right away. Apparently, there's more than one set of Claytons, and a good old-fashioned family feud between the factions."

"Hatfields and McCoys? Shootin' and feudin'?"

"Let's hope not. According to Vincent, the Lucky Lady should have been his father's, but his uncle, that would be late the George, swindled him out of it."

He cast a watchful eye toward the sandbox installed yesterday afternoon where A.J. happily shoveled pale, golden sand onto a bright red fire truck. Gabe's chest filled with overpowering love for his child. Caring for A.J. had kept him anchored when the world had spun out of control.

As if Manny could read his thoughts, he asked, "You found a nanny yet?"

Gabe rubbed a hand over the back of his neck. "There's no daycare here. I've advertised, passed the word around, talked to people, but other than a couple of teenagers, no one has applied."

Manny knew he wouldn't hire a teenager. After Tara and her irresponsible behavior, he would take no chances with his son.

"He's going to the mine with you?"

"What else can I do?"

"Find a young, single, really good-looking nanny."

A quick vision of the pretty woman in the funeral car flashed through Gabe's head. He huffed. "Try older and mature. A.J. could use a grandma type."

Hearing his name, A.J. dropped a handful of sand and toddled to his daddy, face alight with curiosity and pleasure. He was a happy, easygoing kid.

"My juice?" He reached for Gabe's coffee.

"No. Here's your juice." Gabe snagged the sippy cup from the patio table and handed the colorful, cartoon-covered cup to his son. A.J. drank deeply, then dropped the cup and went in pursuit of a black and yellow alpine butterfly. The boy moved so fast, he could be here one minute and gone the next.

Another movement, this one to his left, caught Gabe's eye. He rotated toward the house next door. "Looks like I have a neighbor after all."

The place had been empty since he'd moved to town a few weeks ago, but now a young woman in stretchy jogging pants and a tank top stood on the back porch. She shook the doorknob, then shook it again.

Gabe moved from his leaning post to watch. The woman gave the door a hard yank before moving around to stare up at a window.

This was getting interesting.

"Gotta go, Manny. Either my neighbor has lost her key, or some jogger is trying to break into the house next door."

"I thought you said Clayton was too small for crime."

"No place is that small. I said Clayton seemed a safe place to raise A.J."

"You're not staying down there, Gabe. Don't get any crazy ideas."

Gabe grinned. "Bye, Manny."

"Is she young and beautiful? The pretty ones can be rehabilitated."

"*Bye*, Manny."

Laughing, he ended the call, his focus captured by the young, fit woman doing her level best to climb up the side of the house. She was blond, the kind of pale Nordic blond that cost a fortune to maintain, but the hair was caught up in a casual ponytail. Even from here, Gabe thought she looked pretty, and her outfit showed off curves he didn't want to notice.

If she was a burglar, which he doubted, she wasn't a very good one.

Hoisting A.J. into one arm, Gabe watched for another minute before crossing the lawn. Small towns didn't afford much in the way of entertainment, and the woman was starting to entertain him. The jogger-cum-burglar had one running shoe on the side of the house and was hopping up and down on the other in an effort to catapult herself up to the window frame.

His inner smile grew wider. Yep. Highly entertaining.

She'd just gotten a handhold when Gabe decided to announce his presence. "Morning. Is there a problem over here?"

She gave a sharp yelp. The fingers slipped, rubber sole skittered against siding and the small blonde tumbled down, landing with a thud on her bottom.

"Well."

Gabe went to his haunches. "You all right?"

"Other than the year of life you scared out of me, I'm fine." She put a hand to her heart and Gabe got his first good look at her face. She looked familiar.

"Do I know you?"

"Is this some kind of weird come on?" She cocked an eyebrow at him. "Wait. I saw you in town the other day."

The memory hit him then. She'd been the woman in the funeral car. The one with the sad eyes and lost expression. The one he'd had trouble getting out of his head.

"Maybe," he hedged.

She was younger than he'd thought. Really young with the kind of sweet, innocent look and wide blue eyes that some men found irresistible. Considering her age, he was glad he wasn't one of them…anymore. "Breaking and entering is illegal."

She made a face. It was a cute face, exasperated, embarrassed.

"Not if you're breaking into your own house." She took the hand he offered and hopped up. She was quick and agile like a dancer and in better shape than him. He worked out, but she was much younger and moved like an athlete.

"If this is your house, why are you climbing in a window?"

"I don't have my key."

He jacked an eyebrow. "Locked yourself out?"

"No. I did not." For some reason, the logical question stirred her juices. "I went for a run and when I came back my key was gone," she insisted.

"From your pocket? Maybe you dropped it somewhere on the road."

"The key wasn't in my pocket." Her gaze slid away from his. "I keep one hidden…somewhere. It was there when I left."

"I see." Too stubborn to admit her mistakes.

"Somebody took that key." She fisted a hand on one hip and squinted. The look was comical. Charming, too. "Maybe you took it."

"Me?" Gabe touched his chest, both amused and taken aback at the ridiculous notion. "Why would I steal your house key?"

She surprised him with a laugh. "I have no idea. Dumb thought. Why would a total stranger come walking along and steal my key when I'm out for a jog?" The really cute squint returned. "Unless you're some kind of a stalker."

"How many stalkers do you know that carry

around a two year old? I'm Gabe Wesson, your next-door neighbor. Moved in a few weeks ago." He jerked a thumb toward his house. "This little monkey is my son, A.J."

Everything about her softened—her stance, her expression, even her breathing—as she turned her focus to A.J. Gabe had never seen anyone melt, but he thought his neighbor came close. For Gabe there was nothing more attractive than a woman who liked kids, especially his.

"Hi, A.J." Voice warm, she touched the back of his son's hand with one finger. A.J. responded with his usual babble about trucks and Elmo. "I'm Brooke. Can you say Brooke?"

"Book."

She lifted smiling blue eyes to Gabe's. "He's adorable."

Gabe's gut tightened. So was she. "These days he jabbers constantly. Sometimes I even understand what he's talking about."

"'Book' is pretty close. Lots of kids have trouble with R." As if magnetized by his son, her focus returned to him. She tapped the red toy A.J. clutched against his chest. "What you got there, sweetie? A fire truck? Are you going to be a fireman when you grow up?"

The toddler pointed his chin upward and howled, "Woo-woo-woo."

"That's supposed to be a siren," Gabe said.

"Well, yes. Anyone could recognize that." Amused, she lifted her chin and echoed, "Woo-woo-woo!"

A.J. gurgled with laughter and thrashed the toy against Gabe's chest. "Woo-woo. Firetuck, firetuck."

"Easy there, boy." Gabe caught the truck in one hand. "You're beating up your old man."

Brooke laughed and when she did, a dimple big enough to swim in dented her left cheek. Gabe's belly ker-plopped. He was a sucker for dimples.

A.J. thought the smile was aimed at him and stretched out both arms. The truck dangled from one hand. A.J. was friendly, but he'd always preferred Daddy's arms. Now he bounced and babbled and reached as if Brooke was a long-lost friend.

The action had a curious effect on her. The softened expression became a yearning, but she took one step back and shook her head, setting the ponytail into action. "I'm all sweaty."

"He's all sandy." Gabe lowered A.J. to the grass and wiped a few grains from his shirt.

A.J. toddled over to Brooke and hugged her kneecap. She dropped a hand to the boy's hair. A splint poked out from one finger. No wonder she'd had trouble holding on to the window facing.

"What happened to your finger?"

She glanced down. "Oh. That." The question

seemed to make her uncomfortable. "It's broken. Slammed it in a car door."

"Ouch."

She waved the thick, white-covered splint. "No biggie. It only hurts if I whack it against something." The dimple flashed again. "Which happens way more often than I'd like." With a glance toward the house, she said, "You wouldn't happen to have a skeleton key, would you?"

"Do they still make those?"

"Beats me, but I'll try anything at this point. I've got to get inside."

Gabe grinned. "I'm starting to believe this is really your house."

"Trust me…it is. Why else would I be trying to get inside a place that looks this tired? See that tree over there? If you look real close, you'll notice notches on the trunk. My brother did that after I fell and broke my arm. He was mad."

A broken finger. A broken arm. Like his late wife, she was delicate, breakable, fragile. "At you or the tree?"

"Just mad. That's Zach. Better to attack the tree than the snotty cousin who pushed me."

Gabe gave the statement its due consideration. "I think I like your brother."

"Me, too." She flashed that smile again. "He's a cop."

"Who wouldn't approve of breaking and entering." He cupped his hands. "You don't look like a burglar, anyway. Hop on. I'll lift you up."

"Are you sure?"

He cocked his head, eyebrows raised in amusement. "Only if you're sure you're not a burglar."

She laughed and he got that sinking feeling again in his belly. "You're now my accomplice."

Cute.

After checking the bottom of her shoe and dusting away a couple of chunks of gravel, she gingerly placed a black and pink Nike runner into his laced fingers, steadied herself with a hand on his shoulder and hopped a couple of times to get her momentum.

"Ready?" he asked.

She nodded. "The crime spree begins."

Really cute.

Gabe hoisted and she scrambled up the side of the house like a spider monkey. Gabe stood below, feet braced and arms ready in case she slipped. The athletic Brooke clung to the facing, shoved the window up and tumbled forward with a squeal and a laugh.

Her head poked back out the window. Some of the ponytail had come loose and dangled in her eyes. "Come around to the front. I'll let you in. We'll steal the good silver."

"If someone hasn't already."

She gave a quick look behind her. "Eek!"

Appreciating her humor, Gabe guided A.J. past a showy purple flower bush the falling blonde had barely missed and around to the covered front porch. Elevated three steps up the porch was enclosed an additional three feet by a limestone half wall. A couple of flat-topped pillars stood sentry on either side of the steps. In one corner of the concrete space a green metal chair rusted. A dried-out flowerpot grew cobwebs. Leaves had piled along the edges.

No one had lived here in a while, which made him all the more curious about his new neighbor. She'd come into town for a funeral. Was she staying longer or heading back to where she came from? And why did he care?

A.J. spotted the dangling wind chime and pointed. "Hold you, Daddy," he said, his baby talk indicating the desire to be picked up.

Gabe obliged. Just as A.J. touched the swinging metal discs, the doorknob, an old brass handle that had seen better days, rattled.

"Ta-da." Brooke stood in the open doorway, dimple activated. She swept the bandaged hand over the top of her head and smoothed loose hairs. "Come on in. The coast is clear. If I had a burglar, he didn't take anything...that I know of. You'll have to excuse the place. I just got back last night. My cousin has been looking after things around here, but the house still needs a lot of cleaning."

Gabe and A.J. went inside. Except for a low chair and a couch, the furniture was covered by sheets and the room smelled as musty as an old cellar. "Back from where?"

A shadow crossed her face. "Colorado Springs. I went to college there."

College. She *was* young. "Dropout or graduate?"

"I graduated in May."

"Congratulations." A.J. kicked against his sides. Gabe lowered him to the floor. "So you've come to the metropolis of Clayton to job hunt?"

"Right. Between breaking and entering and directing all that traffic downtown, I'm a busy girl." She indicated the flowered chair. "Sit if you want. I gotta grab a water. Want one? Or coffee? I don't have much in the cupboards yet, but I picked up a few things yesterday, including instant coffee. A little refreshment is the least I can do after you helped further my life of crime."

"We're good. Thanks." He thought about the gourmet coffee he'd abandoned on his back porch and figured getting acquainted with a new neighbor was worth the loss of that specially blended caffeine jolt. He'd never be a snob, but he'd pass on the instant.

"Be back in a jiff." With a dancer's grace, she started out of the living room. A.J. toddled after her.

"Do you mind a shadow?" Gabe called.

She smiled down at his son, that same soft, yearning look he'd noticed before. "No. Come on, A.J. Let's see what Brooke has for you."

Gabe heard the refrigerator open and close, heard her soft voice talking sweetly to A.J. and wondered if she needed a job. A nanny right next door. Not a bad thought. Of course he'd have to check her out but his gut instinct was usually right.

She was one of the Claytons, or at least a friend close enough to attend George's funeral. If she was staying in town—and why else would she return after a trip to Colorado Springs—chances were, she was jobless.

Plus, he liked her. Even if she was a bubblehead who locked herself out and then promptly forgot she'd done so, her sense of humor was attractive. If she was a few years older, he might like her even more.

His fingers tightened on the rough upholstery.

She wasn't older, and he needed to keep that in mind all the time. Never mind that he couldn't stop noticing the dark blue of her eyes or that mile-deep dimple. She was a college girl.

She and A.J. reappeared. His son, the mooch, carried an unpeeled banana.

"Do you mind if he has that?"

"Why would I mind?" he asked.

"You're his dad. Some people do." She curled her legs beneath her on the rust-colored couch and drank deeply from the frosty bottle of water. Gabe tore his gaze away from the smooth, pale neck where a single drop of liquid trickled. She was a college girl. He was a man past thirty with a son to raise and a company to run. Hadn't he learned anything with Tara?

All he needed from a woman was child care.

A.J. thumped the banana against his thigh. "Daddy."

Gabe took A.J.'s banana, stripped down the sides and returned it. "Say 'thank you' to Brooke."

A.J. turned his stellar, gapped-tooth smile on his newest conquest. "Tank oo, Book." He offered the banana. "Bite?"

"No, thank you." She exchanged smiles with Gabe. "Someone is raising him right."

"I'm doing my best. A.J.'s mother died in a car accident." He didn't know why he'd added the last. Maybe because he didn't want anyone to automatically assume he was divorced, although he probably would have been if Tara had survived.

The thought of that last, bitter betrayal curdled in his stomach.

The bottle of water paused at Brooke's lips. "I'm sorry. Raising a baby alone must be really hard."

"Sometimes. Things are tough right now because A.J.'s nanny stayed behind when we moved. Child care's not easy to find in Clayton."

Brooke stilled, her expression part yearning and part fear, neither of which Gabe understood.

"You're looking for a nanny?"

"Would you be interested?" If she said yes, he could ask for references. Or better yet, ask at the Cowboy Café. Hadn't Erin and Kylie mentioned how sweet Brooke Clayton was?

Her eyes widened. "Are you offering me a job?"

"Do you need one?"

"Well—yes, but—no."

He would have laughed but her reaction was strange to say the least. "Can you elaborate a little?"

A.J. angled toward a dangling electric cord. Before Gabe could react, Brooke did. She yanked the plug from the wall and stashed the cord behind the lamp. With a sigh, she leaned one hand on a covered chair and said, "I haven't decided what I'm going to do yet, but I can't work for you."

"Why not?"

"I just can't." A shiny, pink handbag rested on

the end table. She opened the silver clasp and looked inside. Frowning, she bit down on her bottom lip. "I knew that key wouldn't be in here. I put it under the pot, just like always."

She closed the purse with a frustrated *snap*.

Gabe didn't point out that she'd just revealed her secret hiding place. Nor did he point out that she'd dismissed his offer, yet her gaze followed every move A.J. made. Maybe it was best that she'd turned him down. Normally protective of A.J. to the point of paranoia, he wondered what it was about Brooke Clayton that made him trust her. She couldn't even keep up with her keys. But he remembered her face from the funeral and knew he wasn't being fair. She might be a college girl, but she wasn't Tara. Thank God. He didn't know how many times he'd called a locksmith to replace keys or the security company to turn off an alarm his irresponsible wife had triggered. Tara would laugh, peck him on the cheek and call him her hero. The charming, childish ploy had worked for a while, but after A.J.'s birth, Gabe had expected his young wife to grow up. She hadn't.

A.J. high-stepped into Brooke's legs and wrapped his arms around her knees, gurgled something and grinning up at her.

The memory of how close he'd come to losing his son at the hands of A.J.'s own mother froze

Gabe's insides. Never again. No woman, no matter how charming, would ever get the chance to hurt his boy again.

Chapter Three

Brooke noticed the sudden, unexpected change in her new neighbor. One minute he'd asked her to be A.J.'s nanny—an offer that struck her right between the eyes—and the next Gabe had yanked his son into his arms as if the child was in danger.

The notion speared Brooke through the heart.

The little boy was precious. Sturdy body, brown hair and dark eyes that took up a third of his face, and when he laughed, Brooke wanted to snatch him up and nuzzle that soft-looking neck.

Holding a child always put that ache in her chest. The one that reminded her of why she'd never have a baby, of why she'd never pursue a career that involved children, although the desire to do so was eating her up inside.

Gabe resettled in the rose brocade chair Vivienne had bought their late mother early in her successful New York career. A.J. sat on his lap happily smearing banana into his mouth. Whatever had disturbed Gabe couldn't be too serious. He was still here.

Their eyes met, and inexplicably Brooke's stomach fluttered. She felt the same sense of connection she'd experienced the day of the funeral. What was it about Gabe Wesson that intrigued her so?

Certainly, he was handsome, in a dark, scruffy kind of way. He hadn't shaved yet this morning, and his black hair was mussed as if he'd not combed it yet, either. He looked casual and relaxed in worn jeans with his overshirt hanging loose and unbuttoned. Yes, he was good-looking, but it wasn't his looks that drew her.

To circumvent further discussion of the nanny situation, she curled her feet beneath her on the couch and said, "This may seem nosey, but why would anyone leave Denver and move here?"

"Work." He dodged A.J.'s messy hand as the boy tried to poke banana into his mouth. "My company may reopen the Lucky Lady Silver Mine."

His company. Did that mean he was the owner?

"I heard about you a few days ago at my grandfather's funeral. You have the whole town stirred up."

He quirked a brow. "Is that good or bad?"

"Probably both, although nobody really believes there's anything in that mine but bats. If there was, my grandfather would have reopened it long ago."

"You must be George Clayton's granddaughter."

"George Sr., yes," she replied. "My father was George."

"I saw you on the day of the funeral. In the last car. You looked sad."

So he had noticed her, too. Had he felt the same strange sense of connection?

She rubbed a finger and thumb along the sides of the empty water bottle. "I remember feeling sad that no one was sad. Isn't that silly?"

She'd been sad for other reasons that day. The rudderless feeling that came with graduation and the end of college life. The end of her engagement and her plans for the future with no other vision in sight. If not for Grandpa George's bizarre request, Brooke didn't know where she'd be.

"Not silly to me." He shifted A.J. to the chair arm. "Why was no one sad at the funeral?"

"Let's just say George Clayton was not the cuddly kind of grandfather." She thought of how her family had struggled after her father's death. Grandpa George could have helped, but he'd practically turned them out on the street.

"He seemed to be a pretty reasonable man to me."

"You knew him?"

"Briefly, during the mine transaction. Enough to know he made a fair deal and honored all his verbal agreements."

"Maybe he really did find the Lord."

A.J. finished his banana and wiggled down to the worn area rug. Gabe wiped the boy's messy little hands on his own jeans and then let him go. A.J. was off to explore again. He lifted the edges of each sheet covering a piece of furniture, called "Boo" and then giggled.

Someone had played lots of peakaboo with this little doll. She eyed her neighbor. He was watching his son with equal delight, and Brooke found herself attracted even more by the fact that he was a loving father.

She thought she should feel guilty, feeling attraction for a man other than Marty with their breakup only days ago. But the truth was, she didn't. What did that say about her depth of commitment? Maybe she was as shallow as Marty claimed.

She was a little surprised that her next-door neighbor now owned the mine that had belonged to her family for years. Surprised, but not bothered. She considered the old mine worthless.

"You think there's money to be made from the Lucky Lady?"

"My company believes it enough to find out. Since the dollar devalued, silver stock has climbed steadily." He glanced at his son and then back at her. "We believe, by using new mining techniques, the Lucky Lady may prove to be a sound investment."

Brooke knew about as much about stocks as she knew about mining—nothing. "I'm afraid my portfolio is empty at the moment."

If her cousins followed through, the situation was going to change but she'd have to wait a year to find out. In the meantime, she was stuck here with nothing to do but jog and overindulge on Arabella's pastries at the Cowboy Café.

"You can start on that portfolio today. I know you're overqualified, but my job offer stands."

Brooke laughed, though his words struck terror. He was pretty clever about working his way back around to the subject. No wonder he owned a company. "Do most nannies get rich off investments?"

He laughed, too. "Maybe I pay better than most."

"Do you?"

"I could for the right person."

"You don't even know me," she said. "What if I really am a burglar?"

His grin widened. "Are you?"

"No. I'm an international jewel thief searching for the Hope Diamond hidden in this house."

"Under the flowerpot?"

He was making her laugh, and she liked him for

that. She hadn't had much to laugh about the past few days.

"Actually, I don't know what I'm going to do yet. I thought I did. Everything was planned." She loved plans. She loved order. Now everything was out of control, all because Marty changed his mind about being a father. "I was engaged. We broke up."

"Bad deal."

"We were going to do mission's work together and now—" She shrugged. "I don't know why I'm telling you this."

"I don't mind. I'm a pretty good listener."

"Yes, you are." Had Marty ever listened to anything she'd said? Ugh, there she went again, comparing Marty to a man she barely knew. Though the comparison was dead on.

Gabe reached out and poked A.J.'s tummy. The little boy flopped against his dad, dark eyes alight with childish joy. "You can still be a missionary if you want."

That was the trouble. She didn't. All her dreams and plans had been wrapped up in what Marty wanted. "The mission field was Marty's plan, but I didn't know that until we broke up. Helping people, teaching them about Jesus, seemed like a good idea." All those orphaned children in Africa. All those hospitals and schools and orphanages.

"Missions *is* a good idea if it's your calling."

Calling. Had God called her to do anything? "Is your calling to reopen the mine and put this town back on the map?"

"Maybe." He didn't smile when he spoke, and she wondered if he really thought such a thing was possible. Weren't callings only for preachers and missionaries?

"What exactly is going on out at the Lucky Lady?" she asked.

"You should come see for yourself."

"I might. When we were kids we'd sneak out there sometimes and play around. Crazy, I know. The mine has been closed all my life and even with warning signs all around, we were so accustomed to its presence we didn't consider it dangerous."

"But it is. The old-style shafts are poorly supported and the potential for cave-in is real."

"You'll fix that, I suppose," she said.

"If the geologists give us the go-ahead. Right now, we're cleaning and clearing, exploring, determining viability."

"Any work in our little town is exciting."

"I hope everyone agrees with you."

A.J. tried to climb up on the couch next to Brooke. She boosted the diapered bottom, gently dumped him facedown onto the cushions and relished his responding laugh. He looked up, saw her watching and hid his face in the cushions only to peek out again.

"You are such a flirt," she said and tickled his exposed sides. He giggled again, rolled over and pulled his shirt up to expose his round belly.

"Oh, so you want another tickle, huh?" Brooke wiggled tickle fingers above him and made growling sounds. The child cackled, mouth wide, his little hands splayed protectively on his belly as he waited in wide-eyed anticipation. Brooke pounced and A.J. squealed. She tickled gently and when she stopped, A.J. climbed onto her lap and hugged her neck.

A surge of joy filled her chest.

Did Gabe Wesson know how blessed he was?

She opened her mouth to say so but a ringtone cut her off. "Phone, Daddy. Hi, Manny," A.J. said.

With an indulgent smile toward his son, Gabe fished a cell phone from his pocket. After a short, concerned conversation, he rang off. He sat for a moment, quiet and staring as he rubbed his chin in thought.

"I have to run out to the mine."

"Trouble?" Brooke asked.

"I hope not, but we've had some incidents."

He reached for his son, swinging him up and out of Brooke's lap.

"Thanks for the boost through the window. When the real owners arrive, I'll tell them you were my accomplice."

His smile returned. A really nice smile that sent happy waves through her. "What's the punishment for burglary?"

"Life in Clayton, Colorado, without chance of parole." Or one very long year.

"Not too stiff."

That's what he thought. "It was nice meeting you. You and A.J. are welcome anytime."

"Same here. Good to know my neighbors." Gabe started toward the door. "Even if you won't work for me."

At least he was good-natured about her refusal. "Bye now. Thanks, again."

Over his father's shoulder, A.J.'s small fingers beckoned. "Book, come on."

Stunned by the child's request, she lifted a hand. "Bye-bye, A.J."

"No." A.J.'s feet thrashed at Gabe's sides. "Book, come on. Let's go bye-bye. Book!"

Gabe stopped and turned. He shifted the thrashing child into the other well-honed arm. "He's not usually like this."

"He's not?"

"Something about you—" He shook his head. "Would you ride out with us? Keep an eye on A.J.

while I do some troubleshooting?" When she just stood there, he sweetened the pot. "We'll buy your dinner."

Her heart thumped hard.

Couldn't the man take no for an answer?

The Lucky Lady Silver Mine was a giant ant-hill of activity. Men in hard hats and reflective vests carrying clipboards or handheld computers scoured the site. A group of locals she recognized bagged trash while a giant loader scooped debris onto the back of a dump truck. From somewhere came the racket of a drill. Brooke sat in the car with A.J. and watched as Gabe disappeared into a small trailer a few yards south of the old, board-framed mine shaft. The weather was warm so she rolled down the windows, hoping the dust didn't find its way inside.

She was still surprised to find herself here, surprised and nervous. What if something happened? What if A.J. got hurt while in her care? She hadn't been alone with a baby in—not since she was a child.

The horrible memory circled through like a buzzard ready to pluck her heart out.

What was Gabe thinking? She was a virtual stranger. She had no business with his child, but A.J.'s cry had got her moving. She couldn't say no to that sweet request, especially when he was headed for a dangerous construction zone.

She considered getting out of the car to let A.J. walk around, but with all the machinery and activity, she worried. Gabe had parked outside what appeared to be a temporary office, a short distance removed from the actual mine shaft, but she would take no chances.

She unstrapped A.J.'s car seat, crawled into the backseat with him and let him play. Gabe had brought along a bucket filled with toys to keep his son entertained. He also had a DVD player built into the headrest. A.J. promptly dumped out the toys, then began to put them back again. Brooke retrieved the ones that fell to the floor and handed them back. As soon as the pail was filled, he dumped the toys and started over.

"So that's the game," Brooke said when A.J. offered a red block. With some ceremony, she plunked the toy into the plastic bucket. "There you go."

"There you go," he repeated as he added another. He was such a precious, happy little boy Brooke's chest filled with a hot ache just from watching him play.

After a few minutes, he tired of that game and moved on to driving toy cars over the seats and onto Brooke's leg. When she made car noises, he giggled and said, "Do it again."

She did, loving the reward of his belly laugh.

As she fumbled for a fallen pickup truck, she spotted a man heading toward the car. Her stomach sank. The warm pleasure of A.J.'s company dissipated. Her cousin Vincent was not the nicest of her relatives.

He ambled up to the window. "Well, look who we have here. Little Brookey."

Brooke cringed at the snide voice from her childhood. Vincent had teased and tormented her as long as she could remember. Behind the pretty-boy face was a bully who'd gotten into weightlifting for more than sport. He'd used his superior physique and clever mind as weapons. She'd learned to run away or steer clear anytime she saw him.

"Hello, Vincent."

He leaned down to prop his elbows on the window. Muscles bulged in his arms and shoulders. This close, she noticed the slightly crooked nose, the only mar in an otherwise perfect face, broken when Lucas had punched him for calling Mei a derogatory name. "In town for long?"

"Awhile."

"Don't play that game with me, Brooke. I know about the old skinflint's will."

She hitched her chin, not wanting him to see how nervous he made her. Keeping an eye on A.J. was stressful enough without trouble coming around. "My grandfather's will is none of your concern."

"Sure it is. He finally did something right in his miserable life." Vincent laughed, an ugly sound. "Or maybe I should say in his miserable death. We all suspected the old miser had a bankroll. He should have had plenty after he stole everything from my side of the family."

"That was a long time ago, Vincent, and nobody's ever proved he stole anything."

"But we know. Now that we have a chance to get it back, you and the others are not going to stand in the way."

"Is that a threat?" Her nerves quivered. Although not particularly tall, Vincent was ripped. Even before he'd started bodybuilding, he'd known how to intimidate. Behind the handsome face was a self-seeking, devious mind that would stop at nothing to get his way. She glanced at A.J. and wondered what was taking Gabe so long.

"No threat needed, Brookey." He smirked. "The will says you and the rest have to live here a year or my family inherits. Other than doormat Arabella, you're the only one of George's grandkids I see in town."

"You seem to have a lot of information about my grandfather's will."

"Clayton's a small town. People talk." He

glanced over his shoulder at the trailer. "Besides, I'm a Clayton, too. People trust me."

That was probably true. He was gifted at getting his way and letting most people see only what he wanted them to see. She and the other Clayton kids knew the real Vincent.

She turned slightly in the seat, shielding A.J. who continued to play happily. If she ignored Vincent, maybe he'd go away. Please, God.

He reached a finger inside and touched her cheek. Brooke drew back, despising her reflexive cringe. Vincent noticed and his eyes gleamed. "You and I both know none of your side of the family wants to be here. You hate this place. You won't stay. Before you know it, old Vincent will be a wealthy man."

"Aren't you getting way ahead of yourself? If we don't inherit, your grandfather Samuel does. Not you."

"All in the family, darlin'." He bounced a cupped palm against the curve of the window. "Go home to Colorado Springs and paint your toenails, honey. You're going to lose that money. Everything you have is ours anyway."

She remembered the missing house key. Taking it, scaring her a little, was exactly the kind of thing he would do.

"Have you been near my house?"

His lips curved the slightest bit. "Now, honey,

you know where I live. I drive past your house every day."

Eyes narrowed, she asked, "Did you take my key?"

He cocked his head, amused. "Did little Brookey lose her house key? Tsk. Tsk. You should be more careful."

"*House* key? How did you know I was talking about the house key?"

"Must be my ESP kicking in." His white teeth gleamed. He tapped the side of his head. "Oh, and there it goes again. The little voices are saying, 'Run Brookey. Go on back to the city, or you might end up in the creek, too.'"

A cold shudder moved down her spine. She opened her mouth, but no words came. Vincent's words hurt more than they frightened, but they frightened all the same. Greed was a powerful motivator.

To her relief the door to the white trailer opened and Gabe stepped out into the sunshine.

Vincent followed the line of her gaze, saw Gabe and straightened. His demeanor changed with lightning speed as he nodded at the approaching man.

"Boss. Just saying hello to my favorite cousin." The words were so saccharine sweet Brooke's teeth ached from listening. Vincent had missed his calling. He should go to Hollywood and put his good looks and acting talent to good use.

If Gabe noticed the strain on Brooke's face, he didn't let on. "That's right, you two are related. I hadn't made the connection."

"That we are. Used to play together as kids." Right, although Vincent played rough. He was the jerk who'd pushed her out of the tree. "She's been gone a long time. Off to college. Making her mark on the world just like her brother and sister. It's a wonder she's not rich and famous."

Vincent couldn't know how badly the remark cut. Or maybe he did. Vivienne and Zach *had* made their mark. Brooke didn't even have a marker.

By now, A.J. had heard his father's voice and crawled up to the window, arms out. "Daddy, hold you."

When Gabe swung the boy up and out of the car, more of the tension eased from Brooke's shoulders. She'd loved every minute of playing with A.J., but the responsibility weighed heavily. Gabe didn't understand. She wasn't the kind of woman people should trust their kids to.

Vincent chucked A.J. under the chin. When A.J. turned and hid his face in Gabe's shoulder, Brooke smiled. Such a smart little boy.

Vincent shot her a sour look. With Gabe nearby Brooke was feeling brave. Her smile widened.

Her troublesome cousin turned his broad, muscled back to her.

"You look a little worried, Boss," Vincent said. "Is everything all right?"

Gabe frowned and glanced toward the open shaft. "A little problem one of the engineers ran into. We've got it covered." He opened the back door and placed A.J. in his car seat. "I'll be back after lunch. Call me if anything comes up before then."

"Will do. That's what you pay me for." His palm popped the top of the window again. "See you around, Brookey. Good luck finding your key." He winked, then sauntered away.

Chapter Four

Gabe cranked the engine of his Hummer and put the windows up and the A/C on. The blast of cool air was exactly what he needed after the worrisome issue with the equipment. The problem didn't make sense. His people took every safety precaution and his company's tools were top notch. There was no reason for the failure that could have, at the very least, set them back for weeks. At the worst, someone could have been injured. He was proud of Emmanuel Corp's safety record. Nobody got hurt on his watch.

He was still chewing over the situation when Brooke broke into his thoughts. "Does Vincent work for you?"

Gabe glanced at his neighbor. She'd turned slightly in the seat, gnawing at her bottom lip. At some point while he'd been inside the office, she'd taken down her ponytail. The result made his pulse jump. He'd thought she looked young in running clothes with her hair up. What he thought now was that Brooke Clayton was one beautiful woman. Thick waves of pale blond hair fell past her shoulders and set those huge blue eyes off to perfection. He was lousy at describing a pretty woman, but Brooke was like a poem or something.

"What?" he asked, feeling stupid because he'd completely lost his train of thought.

"Vincent. Does he work at the mine?"

"Oh. Vincent." He swallowed. "Part-time. He works at a ranch somewhere, too. Why?"

"You shouldn't trust him, Gabe."

He blinked, surprised at the vehemence in her tone. He was good at reading people and he'd read friction between the cousins even though Vincent had said all the right things. But so far, he'd found Vincent to be a useful employee.

"Care to elaborate?"

"He's not a nice person. You can't trust him."

Which didn't tell him a thing. "He's given me no reason not to."

Her nostrils flared, but she didn't argue. She shifted away, crossed her arms and gazed out the side window, silent.

"I've heard about the bad blood between some of the Claytons. I don't need that kind of trouble on my job site. Vincent's been a big help with the local workforce. I can't complain."

Still, she said nothing. Apparently, the bad blood ran thick and deep and straight into the younger generation. He changed the subject.

"Did A.J. behave himself?"

Her shoulders relaxed a little. "He was great."

"Thanks for riding out with me. I don't like taking him along but—" He shrugged.

She angled her head in his direction.

"I keep trying to hire a nanny," he said pointedly. "And everyone turns me down. I'm getting a complex."

"He's a good child, very easy and sweet natured," she said. "You shouldn't have trouble finding a caregiver, especially this time of year. School's out. High school kids are looking for summer work. Have you asked at the church? Reverend West could probably recommend someone from the youth group."

"Teenagers go back to school. I want someone consistent and mature in his life."

I want you.

His intelligent brain was thumping him upside the head, but his gut and his heart wanted Brooke Clayton. Wanted her for A.J.'s nanny, that is. In the few hours he'd known her, he'd become convinced she was the one, because A.J. had taken to her like a duck to water.

He had, too.

"Hmm. With those requirements, it gets tougher."

Brooke reached over the backseat to do something. Gabe heard A.J. kick his feet in delight and dissolve into gales of laughter. Whatever she'd done had pleased his son to no end.

Gabe dug in his heels. He was a businessman. He ran a corporation. He was a master negotiator. There had to be a way to convince Brooke to work for him, something she needed or wanted that he could supply. "What will it take to change your mind? Name it and it's yours."

Brooke, torso half leaned over the seat, kept right on playing with A.J. "I'm not good with kids."

From the backseat came the sound of a small voice calling for Book.

A scoffing bark of laughter escaped him. "Coulda fooled me."

"I only watched him for a few minutes, Gabe, while you were inside. You have no idea how we'd do alone."

"I just don't get it, Brooke. You like him. He's nuts about you. You need a job and I'm offering to pay you more than most college grads make the first year out." He sighed. "So, what's the deal? Do you think nanny work is below you? Is that it?"

She went silent, but her pained expression puzzled him. Finally, she said, "Please don't think that. I'm complimented, not insulted that you would trust me with A.J. Caring for children is a high calling, an important job. I'm just—I can't. I'm sorry."

All right, he wasn't stupid. He got the message. Probably she wanted to be free to hang out with friends, do her own thing, shop. Like Tara, she was young and wanted to have fun. She didn't want to be tied down to a kid.

Gabe stepped on the gas pedal, feeling the Hummer take hold of the rough, graveled road.

He should be relieved. No need to get involved with another irresponsible woman, even as a nanny.

Then why did he feel so disappointed?

Grandpa George's home was a lovely old Victorian on Grosbeak just off Railroad Street, the main avenue through Clayton. Brooke stood on the big wraparound porch, needing someone to talk to. She hadn't called before coming over. She'd simply shown up, confused and troubled over Gabe's job offer and wondering how she was going to last in this town for a full year. The minivan in the drive was a good indicator Arabella was at home.

As she waited for someone to answer her knock, Brooke gazed around at the home where she'd once spent holidays. The house had been a status symbol to Grandpa, but Grandma had made it warm and cozy yet elegant. Family life had begun to sour after Grandma's death and then fell apart completely after Brooke's father, George Jr. and his brother, Vern, were killed. So many deaths, she thought, beginning with little Lucy who was A.J.'s age when she drowned.

Gabe had been disappointed in her refusal, she could tell, and she felt like an idiot for the way she'd babbled on and on with excuses. He was likely thanking the Lord she'd refused. The truth was, she wanted kids with everything in her, but she couldn't take the chance. Lucy's death had shattered her family. Nothing was worth the risk of that kind of pain again.

A.J.'s bright, smiling face flashed through her mind. She could easily fall in love with a child like him.

"Lord, help me to stand strong. I can't risk it."

She let out a gusty sigh and knocked at the door again.

The memory of Lucy's death still had the power to bring on the black clouds of despair. Lucy was the late baby, the apple of her father's eyes. Brooke remembered wondering why daddy never tossed her into the air or called her his little golden doll. He'd loved Lucy best. They all had, even Brooke most of the time.

Nothing had been the same after her death. Mama had fallen into a depression so deep no one could reach her. She and Daddy had fought at first, laying blame and sobbing in the dark alone. Then they'd simply drifted apart, too miserable to comfort each other. Brooke would never forget some of the things that were said that awful day of Lucy's death and the other things whispered so no one thought she could hear. But she'd known.

Sometimes she wondered why God had let something so tragic happen to their family.

Teeth tight, she shook her head to dispel the thoughts. She'd known this would happen if she returned to Clayton. How would she live like this for a year?

She knocked again. Why didn't someone answer the door?

With determination she grasped for something else to think about. Clayton House was lovely as always, but Arabella had added her crafty hand. The double stain-glassed front doors, embellished with bright sunflower wreaths, shot the afternoon light into dazzling colors. The big porch where Brooke had once played chase with her cousins was adorned with pots of red geraniums, a small, patio-style table and a couple of chairs. A child's baby doll, dressed in a frilly pink dress and bonnet, lay in one of the chairs.

The front door scraped open. "Brooke! Come in."

Brooke followed Arabella into the spacious, formal living room where antique furnishings mixed with the modern clutter of children. Three little girls sat around the coffee table playing tea party.

"Who's who?" Brooke asked, smiling at the four-year-old triplets. They were absolutely precious girls. Arabella's worthless ex-husband had no idea what gifts he'd tossed away like yesterday's garbage. She wondered how her cousin had managed on her own with three small babies, Grandpa George and now a foster daughter. Arabella was a kind a gentle soul to put up with their cantankerous old grandfather, a saint with the strength of a lion. She was beautiful, too, with dark, silky hair and brown eyes, though she probably didn't realize it.

"Everyone asks that," Arabella said with a chuckle. "Jessie is at the end. Jamie's the one with the teddy bear on her lap and Julie has the dirty face. Girls, say hello to Brooke."

Three of the cutest faces, too similar to tell apart, grinned up at her with their daddy's smile and Arabella's brown eyes. "Hi. You like tea?"

The speaker, if Brooke remembered correctly, was Julie. "I love tea. Looks like you girls are having a great tea party. Got any cookies to go with your delicious drink?"

"Uh-huh. We'll share." Jessie carefully placed a vanilla wafer on a tiny plastic saucer adorned in pink princess print and offered it to Brooke. "Mom says we have to."

Brooke laughed. "Thank you, I think. You have lovely manners."

Arabella rolled her eyes. "We're working on those." She indicated the sofa. "Sit down, Brooke. I'm glad to see you back. Are you home for good?"

Brooke nodded, accepting the tea cup and saucer the triplets provided. "Well, let's just say I'm here for the year if I can hold out."

Arabella folded one leg beneath her to sit in the chair next to her triplets. "Have you talked to any of the others since the funeral?"

"Zach and Vivienne. Zach is trying to work things out with his job. Vivienne is still iffy. I'm worried she may not come." With the triplets waiting for her reaction to the "tea," Brooke sipped. "Yum. Which of you made this?"

All three giggled. Dark curls bounced around their cherub faces. "It's water tea."

"The best kind." She nipped the edge of her cookie and, to please her hostesses, moaned appreciatively. The triplets exchanged delighted glances.

"Vivienne has a fabulous life in New York, but I keep praying she'll find a way to take off a year. I worry that Mei was right and we'll have a difficult time getting everyone home for that length of time," Arabella said. "I've tried to call Lucas, but he's not answering."

"Think about it, Arabella. What are we supposed to do in Clayton for an entire year? We need jobs and money to live on until—and if—the inheritance comes." She absently reached over and offered a sip of "tea" to the teddy bear. "I can't imagine living the life of an heiress anyway. I need to be busy."

"Then get a job."

The thought of Gabe's offer loomed large and terrifying. "The Cowboy Café is overloaded with help. The church mostly uses volunteers. Most of the stores are run by the owners and their families."

"People are getting jobs at the old silver mine," Arabella said. "Right now, I think they're hiring mostly men for dirty, cleanup work, but I guess if you're interested in that sort of thing, the manager couldn't discriminate."

"I'm not interested. Besides, the owner, Gabe Wesson, lives next door to me."

Her cousin looked intrigued. "I'd heard he bought Doc Abrams' place. What do you think of him? I've seen him in the café and at church. He seems nice."

Gabe's handsome face flashed before her eyes. "He is."

"Wait a minute." Arabella held up a finger in

thought. "Kylie said Gabe had come into the café asking about a nanny for his little boy. You could do that."

Brooke was already shaking her head. She sat her empty cup on the table. "He asked. I said no."

"Why? Is the little boy a handful or something?"

"Oh, nothing like that. A.J. is absolutely the sweetest thing. Anybody would love caring for him."

Arabella gave her an appraising look. "Then what's the problem? A college degree is not going to do you much good in Clayton. The child is right next door. And the daddy is pretty good-looking, too." Arabella arched a suggestive eyebrow. "The job sounds perfect to me."

Brooke offered her standard line. "I don't do well with kids."

Arabella scoffed. "Get real. You've been playing with Jesse, Jamie and Julie since you arrived."

"That's different."

"How?"

"No, Arabella! I *can't*. Something might happen."

Arabella sat back, awareness dawning. Gently, she said, "That was years ago and you were a child. Let it go."

Brooke glanced away from the piercing, pitying gaze. "I can't."

Julie popped up in front of her. "Mama says, 'Don't say can't. Say you'll try.'"

While Brooke pondered the wisdom of a four year old, footsteps sounded on the staircase. A teenager, dark brown hair swinging around her shoulders, entered the room. Her blue eyes sparkled with a fresh, wholesome prettiness Brooke had noticed the day of the funeral. Even though Jasmine Turner was Arabella's foster daughter and not blood related, she'd come to the funeral and helped with the dinner afterward. Brooke, who'd liked her instantly, gave her extra points for being kind and considerate.

"Hi, Brooke." Jasmine hoisted purse straps over one shoulder.

"Nice to see you again, Jasmine."

"Where are you off to?" Arabella asked, turning toward the teen.

"Cade's taking me for a burger and then we'll probably go hiking or something."

"Oh."

From Arabella's clipped tone and closed expression, Brooke got the feeling Cade, whoever he was, was not popular in this house. "Who's Cade? Anyone I know?" Brooke asked.

Jasmine's chin thrust upward, defensive. "He's my boyfriend, Cade Clayton."

Brooke choked on her vanilla wafer.

"My reaction was the same," Arabella admitted.

"They've been dating awhile, although I've warned her about the other side of the Clayton family."

"Cade's not like them, Arabella. He works hard, and he treats me like a queen."

"I know, honey, I know. It's just that you're both too young. You're barely out of high school. The world is out there waiting." She sighed heavily. "I hate to see you get this involved with a boy at eighteen."

"I love him, Arabella. I can't help it. We won't be out late and you can call my cell if you get worried." She leaned over and kissed Arabella's cheek, wafting the scent of a freshly spritzed cologne. "Good seeing you, Brooke."

Brooke wiggled her fingers. "Same here."

Arabella closed her eyes for a second and took a deep breath. Apparently they'd had this discussion before. "Enjoy yourself, honey. Be careful."

Jasmine blew her another kiss and bounced out of the house, all youth and joy.

"She's dating one of Cousin Charlie's boys?" Brooke was still having trouble with that one.

"She is. He seems like a nice guy, but I'm so worried about her. Regardless of what she thinks now, and how he seems, we both know way more about Great-Uncle Samuel's side of the family than she does. She's convinced they're in love and I'm terrified they'll start making wedding plans any minute." A shadow crossed her face. "I married too young and now I'm struggling to raise these babies alone. I want better for her. I can't see how Cade Clayton can give her anything except a heartache."

"They're both still kids, Arabella. You know how fickle teenagers can be. Probably by autumn the romance will cool, she'll go off to college and you'll have worried for nothing."

"I hope and pray you're right. And speaking of prayer…" Arabella grinned. "How was that for a smooth transition to discussing church?"

"Very clever." Arabella was as solid a Christian as Brooke had ever known, unlike Brooke whose faith was a little shaky most of the time. What had ever made her think she could be a missionary?

"Since you moved away, we've added some great programs. The Bible classes are relevant and interesting, and the Church Care Committee does such good things. We drive the elderly to the grocery store or shop for them, make meals for shut-ins, help with child care for singles. Things like that. If you want to stay busy, you can get involved at church. Are you coming next Sunday?"

"Maybe. Probably." With a sigh, Brooke placed her tiny teacup on the coffee table and stood. What was wrong with a person who couldn't even decide if she wanted to go to church or not? "I should go home. The old place needs a lot of cleaning before I can sleep at night without sneezing."

"I wish I'd had time to keep it up better."

"You did fine, Arabella, and I'm grateful for that much. The place is livable. I can do the rest. Cleaning will keep me from going stir-crazy, at least for a while."

At the front door, Arabella laid a hand on Brooke's arm. "I'm glad you're back. I've missed having family around me."

Brooke's conscience tweaked. Life had been hard for Arabella and she'd handled everything from Grandpa's death to a divorce alone. "Why don't you and the girls come over for lunch tomorrow? Maybe by then I'll have the kitchen sanitized and groceries in the fridge."

"That sounds great, honey, but I'll be working." Arabella baked delectable cakes and pastries for the Cowboy Café.

"You work too much."

"Someone has to feed the three little monkeys." Arabella wiggled Jessie's ponytail. The four year old hugged her mother's side and grinned.

"Yes, but still…" Brooke snapped her fingers. "Hey. Let's plan a spa day. You, me and Jasmine. A girl's day out at Hair Today. While Deanna works her artistry on us, we'll work ours on Jasmine. Who knows, we just might convince her that Mr. Cade is Mr. Wrong."

Arabella's eager expression made Brooke wonder if she ever took time for herself. "My budget is pretty tight. I don't normally spend money at the beauty parlor."

"Which makes a spa day all the more special. My treat. I insist." Okay, now she really needed a job. "Pick a day and I'll call the beauty shop for appointments."

"You know what? That sounds wonderful. I'll look at my calendar and give you a call this evening. Okay?"

"Perfect." Feeling much better than she had when she'd arrived, Brooke gave her cousin a quick hug. "Talk to you later."

As she headed to the door, Arabella's voice stopped her. "As much as I love this idea, I'm pretty sure your financial situation is not much better than mine, Brooke. I think you should reconsider Gabe Wesson's offer. You need to work, and that little boy needs you." When Brooke opened her mouth to protest, Arabella lifted a finger. "No, you listen to me. I'm the oldest and I know stuff." She grinned a little. "Think about that child. He shouldn't be dragged around to a dangerous mining zone. He could get hurt. Then how would you feel?"

Hadn't she thought the same thing? "Oh, Arabella...I don't know..."

"Promise me one thing?"

Brooke smiled. "Because you're the oldest and you know stuff?"

"Exactly, and don't you forget it." Arabella was a gentle soul with the heart of a bulldog. "Pray about that job offer. Pray hard. A mine is a dangerous place for a child."

Brooke nodded and started down the steps toward her car. For the rest of the day Arabella's ominous words rang in her head.

A mine was a dangerous place for child.

Chapter Five

A girl could clean only so much before she went berserk. Or had a lethal allergy attack.

Brooke sneezed as she spritzed furniture polish on the antique armoire in the den and rubbed the golden oak to a shine. The den was one of her favorite places in the house, sprawling and cozy at the same time with glass doors that looked out over the backyard. This time of year Mom's deep blue flower bushes, planted to attract butterflies, were breathtaking. Dad had remodeled the house specifically to create this room. The glass doors had provided a clear view of Brooke and her siblings playing outside while Mom and Dad relaxed in the evenings. Anyway, that's the story she'd been told. The remodeling had come before Lucy.

Now the den seemed empty and lonely, although the furniture remained. A couple of fake Windsor chairs framed the fireplace where she and her siblings had hung their Christmas stockings. Because no one had built a fire in years, she needed to have the chimney cleaned. The ancient candlesticks at each end of the mantel had blackened with age and could use a good polishing, too.

Her mother had loved her silver pieces just as she'd loved all her antiques, but after Dad's death she had sold most to pay debts, replacing them with a few fake pieces and other furniture sturdy enough to withstand the rigors of three adolescents. Brooke was glad the candlesticks and the armoire had survived. The house and its contents were a bittersweet reminder of everything her family had suffered and lost.

Grandpa George's inheritance money would have meant much more ten years ago after Brooke's father died. Mother had needed help badly, but her grandfather had never let on about his vast wealth. Part of her wanted to be bitter about that.

She had a quick flash of the day she, Zach and Vivienne had buried Mother. Barely out of high school, she'd been dumbstruck with grief. Grandpa George had not attended the church service but he'd come to the cemetery, his face haggard and gray. Afterward he'd come to her, Sinatra-style fedora in hand, and murmured, "Your mother was a fine woman. She endured when others didn't."

Though Brooke hadn't completely understood the meaning, the words were the kindest she'd ever heard from Grandpa's lips. At the time, they'd comforted her broken heart, and she'd been grateful. His kindness proved, she supposed, that there was good in everyone, even George Clayton, Sr.

"Well, Grandpa, there's the one good memory." Perhaps if she focused on that single comment, she'd feel less bitter about the things he could have done and hadn't. Maybe.

She set the spray can on the floor and opened the doors to the armoire. The musty smell of old books filled her nostrils. A spider scampered up the door facing. Brooke smashed it with the dust cloth. The dust in the downstairs rooms had started to relent but cobwebs and spiders hadn't. She hated spiders.

With a shudder, Brooke reached into the cabinet and took out the contents to clean inside. Once done, she turned her attention to the stack of books, photo albums and newspaper clippings on the floor. They were crisp and yellowed and probably full of spiders. Still, she slid cross-legged to the floor and began to sort and dust.

"Today the den. Tomorrow the living room." Eventually, she'd clean out the bedrooms, with the hope that Zach and Vivienne would come home to occupy them. The master bedroom with the connected bath would be great for Zach. Viv could have Zach's old room. Lucy's room remained a clutter of storage because Mother never wanted to change a thing after her death. Brooke certainly didn't want to sleep in there and was glad for the downstairs room she'd once shared with Vivienne. Eventually, she might eliminate the musty, wet-wood scent in her old room.

She checked her watch. The locksmith—actually Henry Johnson, the local handyman and plumber—had promised to drop by sometime today and change her door locks. After talking to Vincent, she knew he'd taken her key. He was probably just trying to intimidate her, but she was taking no chances.

She stacked books from the armoire to one side and laid the photo albums out on the floor in chronological order, wiping away dirt and grime. Then she turned each up by the binder to shake out any resident spiders and bugs. Several photos trickled to the wood floor. Zach in his football uniform scowled from one, his game face on. Brooke smiled, remembering how he'd growled and slammed his body into walls to "warm up" before a big game.

She opened the album to replace the photo. Gut-punched, her breath whooshed out. "Lucy."

Her baby sister's angelic face smiled up at the camera. On her father's lap, Lucy pretended to read an oversize children's book.

A fist closed around Brooke's heart. This was taken before the world as her family knew it had ended.

Suddenly, she wanted to remember her family as they had been when they were happy. She started at the beginning, thumbing slowly through each book. There were her parents, George Jr. and Marion, smiling and in love at a beautiful wedding and honeymoon in Hawaii. Then came the births of Zach, Vivienne and herself, and still her parents smiled, arms around each other. She flipped through years of school photos, Christmases at the Clayton House, birthday parties, and then there was her mother, round and expectant with the last baby, Lucy.

For a child who'd lived less than three years, Lucy had been photographed more than all of them. She was beautiful, a joyful, giggling doll, the hands-down family favorite. Like a painter's dream, she had enormous blue eyes in a heart-shaped face and a wild fluff of long, golden curls.

Brooke's chest ached as she turned pages. She'd loved her baby-doll sister with all the passion an eight year old could muster. But she'd been jealous, too. For six years, she'd been the baby until Lucy had come along.

There was Dad giving Lucy a piggyback ride. A water-splashed Mom giving Lucy a bath. Dad, arms out, waiting to catch Lucy as she toddled her first steps.

A Christmas photo the year Lucy turned two showed a big, happy family celebrating right here in this room beneath a tree laden with gifts. Brooke remembered that Christmas. They'd all dressed in their Christmas best and gone to Denver to have a group portrait made. Mom had sent out dozens of embossed, photo Christmas cards from "George Jr., Marion and family." It was the last time they'd ever taken a family photograph.

There had been happiness in this home once. The evidence was here on these pages.

The last book, though, was different. Life had changed. Lucy was gone. As Brooke turned the pages, she didn't find one photo of her parents. She knew why, of course. The family was shattered. Sadness had come to live in George Jr.'s home. Pictures were empty without Lucy's joyful glow.

Rationally, Brooke knew Lucy's death was not her fault. She'd been a child, too, but she could still hear her mother's screams inside her head and her father's furious demands to know what had happened. Why hadn't Marion been with Lucy?

The answer was always the same. Brooke was supposed to be watching her.

Brooke slammed the book closed and sat in the middle of the floor, still grieving something that happened fifteen years ago.

"Why, Lord? Why did it happen? Why can't I move on?"

The old house echoed once and then fell silent again.

She'd ask the questions before and gotten the same answer. Nothing.

Lonely, sad and full of memories, Brooke cleaned each binder and slowly put everything back into the armoire.

What she needed was a good gym workout or a swimming pool. A dozen laps would shake off the melancholy.

But there was no pool in Clayton and the only gym belonged to the school.

With a quiet click, the only sound in the rambling house, she closed the armoire door and headed to the kitchen.

She washed the dust from her hands, chugged water to quench her thirst and considered taking another run. The idea of a year without a health club made her crazy.

At times like this, she wondered if she could really do this. Was an inheritance worth a year in Clayton surrounded by relatives who didn't like her and too-vivid memories?

Her cell phone vibrated against the kitchen counter. She unplugged it from the charger and answered. "Hello."

A woman's muffled voice said, "Brooke."

Brooke glanced at the caller ID and saw, *Unavailable.* "I think we have a bad connection. I can barely hear you."

The muffled voice deepened to a harsh whisper. "You're not welcome here. Go away."

Goose bumps quivered down Brooke's spine. "Who is this?"

"Did you find your key?" the voice rasped. "Be careful. Something could happen."

Brooke rushed to the window over the kitchen sink and looked outside. All she could see was Gabe Wesson's house.

"Who is this? What do you know about my key?" Her fingers trembled. The bandaged splint, dusty from cleaning, clicked against the plastic phone.

"Leave now—" the voice drew out each word in an eerie threat "—if you know what's good for you."

Then the line went dead.

Brooke leaned against the counter, her pulse thrumming fast enough to lap the track at Indianapolis. Her first thought was Vincent, but the caller had been a woman. Cousin Marsha, then, Vincent's sister. They'd always flocked together like vultures waiting to peck out an eye. Now, they'd do anything to inherit Grandpa's money. *Anything.* That was the scary part. If any of Great-Uncle Samuel's bunch of mischief-makers wanted to cause trouble, they were mean enough to do it.

She shivered, suddenly very alone in the big, old two-story house.

Her family's home was at the edge of town with no other homes behind. Someone could come up through the woods, across the creek and into the yard without her seeing a thing. And someone had a key to this house.

Brooke's imagination took flight.

Shaking, she stuffed the phone in her pocket. Was someone watching her every move?

A hot shower was a fine invention.

Gabe rubbed a towel over his damp hair and then shrugged into his shirt. On the couch next to him, also fresh from the shower, A.J. waited patiently for his father's attention.

"You need a comb, little man."

"I got comb." A.J. whacked the side of his head with a hairbrush in an attempt to groom himself. Gabe chuckled, scooped the boy onto his lap and took the brush.

"You need a haircut, don't you?"

"No." No and mine were A.J.'s favorite words.

"Yes, you do. Do you think there's a barber in Clayton?"

"No." A.J. wiggled down and headed for his toy

four-wheeler. When Gabe didn't follow, A.J. turned back. "Come on, Daddy. Let's pay outside."

A.J. loved outside. He'd stay out all day if someone had the patience and time to watch him.

"So much for your early bath," Gabe muttered, but he took the riding toy in one hand and offered the other to his son. He'd endured a long, busy day. Some down time in the quiet backyard sounded good to him, too. "Out we go."

In a jitterbug of excitement, A.J. gave a little scream and pumped his short legs up and down. "Outside," he yelled and raced for the door.

Just as Gabe set the mini-ATV on the porch, he saw Brooke Clayton come around the corner of her house, moving rapidly toward her parked Toyota. Something in her body language held his attention. She kept looking around as if someone was chasing her. Stiff, rushed, head turning left and right, she looked…scared.

He walked to the end of the porch. "Brooke, everything okay?"

She spun around, hand to her throat. When she saw him, she wilted. "Gabe. You scared me."

While maintaining a clear view of his son, he started toward her. "That's two I owe you."

"What?" Her face was smudged with dirt and pale as paste.

Gabe frowned. Something was not right here. "Never mind. Are you okay? You look upset."

Her huge blue eyes grew wider. "Where's A.J.? Don't leave A.J. alone."

"A.J.'s right there. See?" He angled his body to give her a clear view.

She blew out a long sigh. "Of course he is. I'm sorry. I should go."

"Hey." He caught her arm. "You're shaking. What's going on?"

Part of his brain said to mind his own business, but Gabe had trouble doing that. Manny called him Lancelot because he had a knack for stumbling into people, usually women, who needed help. How did a man walk away when a woman needed him? Wasn't that why God made male and female? So they could help each other? Hadn't God given man instructions to take care of the woman?

Right, he thought grimly—caring for the last one had nearly cost him his son.

"I had a scary moment. That's all." She shuddered. "Big, old empty houses. I'm fine now."

Gabe squinted, thinking there was more to this than getting spooked in an empty house. She was *not* fine.

Go back to your porch, Gabe. Let it go. That's what his brain was saying, but his mouth said, "Anything I can do?"

She weighed the offer, her bottom lip caught between her teeth. He wished she wouldn't call attention to the fact that her mouth was full and soft and curved upward at the corners.

"Would you mind some company?" she asked. "I'm sorry. I don't usually impose on new acquaintances, but I'd rather not be alone right now."

Yep. Something was going on, though he wondered why she didn't tell him. He did a quick appraisal of her house and saw nothing out of the ordinary.

"No imposition. We're neighbors. Neighbors help each other. Remember? You helped me out with A.J. the other day. Come on over. A.J. and I are chillin' out after a long day."

She fell into step beside him. "I appreciate this."

Her breath was still shaky and he waited again for her to tell him what was troubling her. She didn't, so he asked, "Have you had dinner?"

She shook her head, still preoccupied with something. The cynic in him wondered if she'd lost her keys again or overdrawn her bank account, but his gut felt differently. This wasn't an airheaded moment. She'd been afraid when he'd first seen her. And she was still nervous.

"I was thinking about getting a burger at the Cowboy Café," she said.

Gabe pointed toward the charcoal grill at one end of his back porch. "I'm thinking club steak and fresh corn on the grill."

Her dimple flashed. "I like the way you think."

"That's better," he said. "For a minute, I thought you'd lost your sense of humor."

"I had," she said.

"Are you back?"

"I think a steak and fresh corn might fix me up."

Gabe grinned. Nothing like a woman who knew how to joke.

When A.J. saw their approach, he threw a leg over the four-wheeler so fast he nearly fell. He ran forward, mouth open wide, chattering a long, garbled sentence that ended with, "Book! Hi. Hi. Come pay outside."

Brooke went to a crouch and A.J. slammed into her, short arms going around her neck. Gabe watched while Brooke's eyes closed and her lips curved in a soft smile as if holding A.J. was the most wonderful thing in the world. A.J. was wild about her, and unless he was way off, Brooke felt the same about the boy. He wished he could find a way to change her mind about the nanny job.

She stood, bringing A.J. up with her. The boy pointed to the bandage on his arm.

"No Elmo," he said.

Brooke raised a questioning eyebrow at Gabe.

"No Elmo," he repeated. "There's no Elmo on the bandage. He has Cookie, Ernie and Bert, but no Elmo."

Brooke squinted at the bandage. "Well," she said in an ultra-serious voice. "What happened to Elmo?"

A.J. lifted both hands in a baby shrug. "Elmo went bye-bye."

"I take it Elmo is his favorite?" she asked, amused.

"Hands down. Ranks right up there with Buzz Lightyear." Gabe hitched his chin toward the umbrella-covered table to the right of the porch. "There or here?"

"Either. It's really nice outside today." She let a wiggly A.J. down with a final hug. A.J. made a beeline for his ATV, hopped on and pressed the button, and with herky-jerky motion, he puttered the length of the porch. "Do you grill much? If you say yes, you may have company all the time."

Gabe wondered if that would be a good thing or a bad thing, considering how he couldn't stop sneaking glances at his new neighbor. Today she wore a long, sky-blue T-shirt over a pair of trendy jeans, the kind with rips strategically placed for best effect. He'd never pay good money for a pair of torn jeans, a reminder that he and Brooke came from different generations. She looked like what she was—a fresh-faced college grad with the world in front of her while he was already worn around the edges—like her jeans.

With an inward sigh and a swift kick in the mental pants, he opened the metal grill lid and checked for cleanliness. Sometimes he got caught up in work or A.J. and forgot to scrub. "A grill's a bachelor's best friend if he likes to eat at home."

"When I was small my dad used to grill in the back yard in the summers." She pointed to the space that was now overgrown with flower bushes, grass and other unidentifiable plants. No grilling apparatus was anywhere to be seen. "The smell of those hamburgers lured every dog for miles around and a few nearby neighbors. Mmm. So good…"

A nostalgic smile spread across her face. "While Dad cooked and Mom brought out the dishes and fresh vegetables, all three of us kids ran around, kicking a ball or playing chase. Sometimes one of us would grab Dad's water bottle and squirt the other—usually my brother Zach—then the war was on."

"Sounds fun." A lot more fun and playful than his own childhood. Brooke was a Clayton in a town owned by Claytons. Gabe Wesson had been the son of a poor, uneducated laborer who worked such long hours he was never home to grill anything. Later, after Dad's death, life had been even harder.

He glanced across at Brooke's family home, still nice in a tired way even though the house had sat empty for a while, and compared the two-story house to the run-down apartments in the poor neighborhoods of Denver where he'd grown up. She'd lived a charmed life while he was attending high school by day and working thirty-hour weeks to put food on the table for his mother and sisters. No wonder she seemed like a spoiled princess to him. Like Tara.

Still, he wasn't complaining. God had blessed him. His hard work had paid off and his mother no longer had to work two or three jobs. She didn't have to work at all if she didn't want to.

"Sounds like you had a great family." A.J. wheeled past, the motor humming. Gabe swept the boy off the vehicle with one arm. "Come on, little man. Gotta go inside for minute."

"No, Daddy. I play."

Gabe ignored the expected protest and opened the back entrance, standing aside for Brooke to enter.

She took hold of the door and let him go first, then followed him through the back door into the giant, modern kitchen. "What about your family? Any brothers or sisters?"

"Two sisters, both younger. They live in Denver."

"Did you torment them when they were small?"

"What do you think?" he smirked.

Brooke laughed, shooting that dimple at him. "Are all big brothers pests?"

"Pests and protectors. It's in the male chromosome."

"Oh, I hear that. Zach would tease Vivienne and me until we screamed but if anyone else bothered us, look out!" She grinned. "What about your mother and father? Are they in Denver, too?"

"Mom is. Dad died when I was fourteen."

She tilted her head. "My dad died when I was a teenager, too. Thirteen."

"No kidding?" His empathy meter rose. "Losing a father is tough on a kid."

"He and my uncle were both killed in the same accident." She gave a slow shake of her head. "The entire town was in shock for a long time. The hardest part came after the shock wore off."

"Yes. I remember." Because of the shared grief, he felt a special connection with her beyond the buzz of attraction and the determination to make her A.J.'s nanny. Maybe she wasn't a spoiled princess after all. She'd had her share of sorrow, just as he had. "My dad was a good man who worked hard but he never made much money. He used to joke that he was worth more dead than alive."

"He was so wrong."

"Oh, yes. He was wrong. In more ways than one." There had been nothing but a pitifully small Social Security check to take the place of his father. "He was on a construction site when a pipe fell. He pushed a coworker out of the way."

"A real-life hero, Gabe," she said sincerely. "You can be proud of that."

He was now, and more than anything he wanted to make his father proud in return, but back then, not so much. "The irony is, he'd taught a Sunday school lesson on the importance of putting others first, of imitating Christ by being willing to lay down your life for others. Most people considered the teaching a metaphor of sorts, I think, but Dad lived what he believed. Me? I was just a kid who wanted my father back."

"I know." She leaned against the granite counter, watching A.J. as they talked. "Do you think A.J. will ever yearn for his mother the way we did our fathers?"

"He was really small when she died, but I've wondered about that, too. I don't want him to feel as if he's missed out on a mother's love, but—" his eyes followed the happy, playing toddler "—what can I do?"

"Does he spend time with your mother and sisters?"

"When we can work it out. They'd keep him all the time if they could, but I want him with me. Sometimes I wonder if I did the right thing by moving to Clayton instead of staying in Denver near them."

"Why not go back to Denver? Send someone else to open the mine."

Gabe rubbed the center of his chest with the tips of two fingers. "Something in here. Prayer. God. I can't explain it, but we're supposed to be in Clayton." Before she could laugh or ask if he was crazy, Gabe turned away and took three plates and a platter from the cabinets. "Can you make a salad?"

Brooke pushed away from the counter and came to his side. "I'm not a sous-chef like my sister, but I can cut up lettuce and tomatoes."

"Knives are in that drawer. Bowls are up there." He pointed as he removed steaks from the freezer, then popped them into the microwave to thaw.

A.J. dragged a toy computer and a chunky truck into the kitchen. The truck clattered onto the natural stone tile and the toddler followed it down. Brooke bent to press a button on the computer and activated the ABC song. A.J. patted his hands and sang along.

Gabe hadn't been in a kitchen with an unrelated woman in a long time, but he was glad to be here with Brooke. He liked watching her with A.J. He liked joking with her and hearing her giggle, though the sound reminded him of her age. He even liked the hum in his blood he'd thought had died long before Tara did.

Coming back to life was both pleasure and

discomfort. As much as he tried to pretend that he wasn't attracted to Brooke Clayton, he was.

For A.J.'s sake and his own, he'd have to be very careful.

Chapter Six

"This is amazing." Brooke leaned back in her patio chair with a deeply satisfied sigh. "I've never had corn like this before."

With A.J. in a booster chair between them, Brooke and Gabe finished off their impromptu backyard cookout. For the past hour, they'd talked. The sun had slipped behind the mountains a few minutes ago and silvery gray twilight shimmered around them.

She'd told him about the inheritance. He'd told her about the mine and his vision of resurrecting the dying town of Clayton with a shot in its economic arm. She'd told him about the town and the people, about her siblings and growing up here. She'd even told him about her grandfather's will.

Gabe Wesson was an easy man to talk to. He listened as though he'd remember, something Marty had never done—though she'd reminded herself more than once that Gabe was her neighbor, a nice widower with a son, not her college boyfriend.

Still, there was something shimmering in the dusky evening air, in the occasional tease and laugh and quick glance, that indicated more than friendly neighbors.

"I think A.J.'s getting sleepy," Gabe said with a hitch of his chin toward the toddler whose head bobbed and his eyelids drooped. "Ready for bed, little man?"

A.J. jerked to attention, eyelids batting to stay awake. "No."

Both adults laughed. Brooke had never seen a better father than Gabe. He was the perfect mix of tender and tough. Though he was doing a great job with his son, Brooke's heart hurt a little to think of the boy as motherless. Even with all the problems in her home after Lucy's death, Brooke couldn't imagine not having a mother. Surely, a man like Gabe would remarry someday. Would a stepmother love this precious baby the way he deserved?

Without stopping to think of all the reasons she shouldn't, Brooke let instinct take over. She pulled A.J. onto her lap and began to rock. "He's tired. When is his bedtime?"

Gabe glanced at his watch. "Fifteen minutes ago."

A.J. snuggled against her T-shirt and sighed.

Brooke's heart squeezed. Given half a chance, she could fall in love with her neighbor's son. The yearning inside to have and to love a child grew every time she saw him. She looked up at Gabe. He watched her rocking his son with a curious expression on his face. Brooke suddenly had the bizarre thought that she could fall in love with the father, too. This time her heart dipped, falling with a sick thud to the pit of her stomach. She must be going crazy. All the stress of the past week had loosened a screw in her head. She barely knew Gabe Wesson.

"Mind if I ask you something personal?"

A nerve inside Brooke jerked. "Go ahead."

"Even if the inheritance works out, don't you want to use your degree? Don't you want more out of life than money?"

"Interesting that you should ask because I've been mulling that very thing," she said, rocking back and forth, one hand cradling A.J.'s head, the other his back. "I don't really want to be an heiress. Not that I can't use the money, but the idea of doing nothing holds no appeal. I like goals. Plans."

"What do you want? Tell me about your goals and plans," he asked, his deep voice a quiet rumble in the settling dusk.

"I don't have any."

"Come on. Everyone has a dream. I told you one of mine. Now you tell me yours."

Her dream was impossible. A baby to love, kids in her life. "I'd once thought about teaching, maybe coaching. But that's out."

"Why?"

"Wrong degree." She didn't tell him she'd intentionally taken the wrong classes. Even if she taught someone else's children, she'd be taking a chance. One of the reasons she'd dated Marty was the ridiculous hope that she could ride shotgun with him in the orphanages and day camps without risking anything.

Maybe that was her problem. She was afraid to risk just as she was afraid to get too involved with a child.

"You're young. If you want to teach, you could go back to college."

She pretended to shudder. "Please. I barely squeaked by as it was. I'm not going back." Brooke, the C student. Brooke, the queen of blowing off classes. "I'd thought about working in one of those Y kind of places where kids do camps and learn to swim or play ball."

"I can see that. You're athletic. Energetic. Great with kids."

A lot he knew. "That's the problem." When he raised his eyebrows, she tried to explain, though sometimes her reasoning didn't make sense to herself. So how could she make someone else understand? "The whole kid thing. That's why my boyfriend and I broke up. He wanted kids. I didn't."

A.J. gave a quivering sigh and snuggled deeper as if challenging the lie. Brooke's throat tightened with emotion. She'd made the claim for such a long time she'd begun to believe it. Avoidance was her standard line of self-defense. By denying she wanted children, she could avoid the risk of hurt. Now, with A.J. in her arms and Gabe staring at her with dark, curious eyes, her standard line didn't seem as convincing.

The tiki torches lit to discourage mosquitoes cast Gabe in alluring shadows. He looked dark and attractive, strong and secure and all man. He also looked bewildered. And why shouldn't he? She'd chosen to rock his son, chosen to stroke the baby-soft skin over and over with her fingers as though touching him was life itself.

"Do you realize how contradictory that is? You wanted to be a teacher, you want to work with kids in a rec center, but you don't want children personally. I'm lost here."

Oh, so was she. Unbelievably lost.

"It's not that I don't like children..." she floundered.

"What are you afraid of, Brooke?" Gabe's quiet baritone spoke right to the issue, honest and piercing.

Brooke looked away toward the hulking shape

of the mountains, deep purple now in the growing darkness. She swallowed, aching, needing release from the pain that knotted beneath her breastbone and refused to let go. The knot had started years ago as she stood on the banks of Silver Creek, screaming for Lucy, and year after year, the knot had tightened until at times, like now, the noose threatened to squeeze her in two.

She *was* afraid. Terrified. She'd planned her life around keeping her heart safe, never, ever planning to have children. A husband was okay as long as he agreed to the child ban. She'd intended to stay on the periphery, a safe extension of Marty's ministry to the orphans and needy of the world, close but not too close. Wouldn't that be enough to please God? To repay the harm an eight year old had done to the people she'd loved most?

"It's complicated." Her voice was quiet, too, an aching whisper.

"I'm listening."

She rarely spoke of Lucy's death and the horrible aftermath of watching her family disintegrate. She'd told Marty, only to have her sorrow flung back in her face in anger and impatience. "Grow up. Get over it. Stop whining about something that happened fifteen years ago." The hurt of Marty's words still stung. She liked Gabe and A.J. too much to take the risk of having the same thing happen again.

"Something happened a long time ago." The knot in her rib cage tightened. Rising, she shifted A.J. to one shoulder, careful not to wake him. The heat of his body contrasted with the rapidly cooling air. "Shouldn't we take him to his bed? The night's getting cool."

To Gabe's credit, he didn't press, but rose with her. He stepped closer, stirring the scents of charcoal and aftershave. "I'll take him."

"We're fine." Brooke nodded toward the back door. "Lead the way."

She followed him through the kitchen and a tidy, masculine living room down a hallway to a child's bedroom. Gabe flipped on lights as they went.

"Watch your step," he said quietly as he moved across to turn back the bed. A jumble of toys littered the floor. "No matter how many times we pick them up, he gets them out again."

Brooke gently lowered A.J. to the sheets. She was amazed to find the room was clean at all. How did Gabe have the time to work, care for a toddler and keep a house semi-clean? He must be exhausted. A twinge of guilt pinched her. He needed help. He'd asked for it. No one, including her, had stepped up to the plate.

"I'll get his shoes," she whispered and slipped off the pair of brown sandals while Gabe efficiently wrestled the child into pajamas. When A.J. stirred and mumbled, Gabe paused, waited for him to settle, then pulled the sheet up to the small chest. Squiggly curls stuck to the sides of A.J.'s head where he'd sweated against Brooke. Gabe smoothed them as he kissed his son's forehead.

Brooke observed the sweet, unself-conscious action of a father who loved his child and wasn't afraid to show affection. She doubted if Gabe Wesson was afraid of anything.

"You're a great dad," she whispered.

They were standing side by side, gazing down at the sleeping child. Gabe shifted, swiveling slowly toward her.

"Thanks." Coffee-brown eyes caught hers and held. Maybe it was the intimacy of the situation, standing next to the sleeping baby. Maybe it was the relaxed and comfortable mood of a pleasant evening shared. But some indiscernible feeling passed between them, an emotion ripe with possibility.

The thought leaped into Brooke's head that she'd like to walk into Gabe's arms and lean her cheek against his chest, to be secure in those strong, muscled arms.

She took a step back, startled by the intensity.

"I should go," she said.

The feeling dissipated like the ghostly gray

mists of dawn, leaving Brooke to wonder if she'd imagined it.

As she crossed the lawn toward her darkened house, Gabe stood on the porch, waiting until she was inside. When she flipped the light on and waved from the back porch, he lifted a hand and disappeared.

Brooke glanced around the quiet, empty and almost-clean den. When she'd run out of this house hours ago, she'd been afraid. Now, she felt perfectly safe, and the reason was clear. Gabe Wesson was next door, a man she instinctively trusted, a man whose presence made her feel secure. Though she'd only known him a few days, Brooke knew without a doubt that if she needed Gabe, he would come.

With the extra house key still missing, she slid a chair under each doorknob, though she was no longer nervous about being alone in her family home. The locksmith would surely come tomorrow. She'd be fine tonight.

As she headed for the shower, she thought about that sweet moment in A.J.'s room. She'd never put a child to bed before. She'd never rocked a toddler until he fell asleep. She'd never stood beside a man and watched him kiss his son good-night.

Oh, the simple, beautiful joys.

Did Gabe have any idea of how special that

time had been to her? Of how she'd been touched and challenged?

More important, what was she going to do about any of it?

Gabe moved quietly down the hall to take a final peak into A.J.'s room before turning in. He paused in the doorway, his chest filled with overpowering, helpless love. Sometimes he lay awake at night worrying that something would steal this gift from him. Nothing in his life had ever had the ability to make him afraid the way A.J. did. He'd spent a lot of time with God, praying through the fear and anxiety of being a single parent, but it always returned, usually in his sleep or in that twilight time between sleep and consciousness. A fear would grip his heart and squeeze the breath from him.

He understood Brooke's fear, though she'd told him nothing about the reasons. He understood because he was afraid, too. Since the tragedy that had claimed Tara and nearly stolen A.J., the anxiety returned again and again, but with the Lord's help he'd learned to simply keep moving forward. What choice did he have? He had a son. He had a business. He had dozens of employees and a mother depending on him.

That was the key to his success in everything. Pray hard and then do it afraid.

He shook his head and padded down the hall to his own bedroom. This room was very different from the one he'd shared with Tara. He'd lived in a frilly, messy fairy tale with Tara's clothes strung from one end of the room to the other, her cosmetics left open, her perfumes strong enough to cling to his suits and jeans. When he'd tired of Manny's teasing, he'd sent his clothes to the cleaners, then moved them to another room. Tara had pouted, but her pouts lasted only until she'd wrangled another shopping trip out of him.

Shopping. She'd once left A.J. in his crib while she went shoe shopping. When he'd come home to find the baby alone and crying, he'd gone ballistic. Tara claimed she'd forgotten. Worse, she'd asked what was the big deal? It wasn't like A.J. could walk or anything. He was safe in his crib.

How did a mother forget about her child?

He pushed up from the bed and went down the hall to A.J.'s room, needing reassurance one more time that all was well. A.J.'s chest rose and fell in gentle rhythm.

"Thank You, Lord. Protect him when I can't."

He lingered in the doorway, watching his son, listening to the gentle breathing.

Something had happened tonight with Brooke Clayton. He'd known he was attracted to her and didn't want to be. Tonight, when they'd stood together next to A.J., a strange family feeling had come over him. Maybe he'd been alone too long. Certainly Brooke was too young for him, too young to even know what she wanted to do with her life.

But on some deep level, he and Brooke had connected.

Gabe couldn't get that feeling out of his head.

The telephone shook Brooke from a solid REM sleep. She grappled for the tiny cell phone somewhere on the bedside table, made contact and pulled it onto the pillow next to her ear.

"'Lo." Her voice sounded like a gravel grinder.

"Brooke, I hope I didn't wake you."

"Gabe?"

"You were asleep."

She squinted at the cell phone's white illuminated display. She'd been asleep for only thirty minutes? Rapidly blinking away the cobwebs, she cleared her throat. "No problem. I just got in bed. Is something wrong?"

"There was an accident at the mine."

She sat straight up, the sheet falling to her waist. "Is anyone hurt?"

"I don't know. We aren't working night shifts, so I'm not sure what's going on. I got a call from the sheriff. He said there was an accident and they need me there."

The reason for his call dawned as Brooke tossed

back the sheet and swung her feet to the chilly floor. Even in early summer, a Colorado night was cold. "What can I do?"

"Will you come over and stay with A.J.? I'm sorry to have to ask, but I hate to drag him out of bed this late. He's sleeping soundly. He won't be a bother."

She could hear his frustration. His responsibility to his son warred with the responsibility of running a business.

"What if something happens?" she asked, head too muzzy from sleep not to speak her mind. He was asking her to be alone with A.J. for an indefinite period of time.

"What could happen, Brooke? He's asleep. You can sleep, too, if you want."

Sleep? While caring for a child? If the statement wasn't so frightening, she would have laughed.

But how could she refuse? What kind of hateful, self-centered person would say no to such a plea? A little child needed uninterrupted sleep. If Gabe woke him, A.J. would be tired and cranky. He'd cry. He'd be miserable. How could Gabe investigate the problem at the mine while tending to a fussy child? Surely, she could do this—once—for a man who'd come to her rescue twice in the space of a week.

Before all the reasons she shouldn't could rush in and stop her, Brooke took a trembling breath and said, "I'll be right over."

Chapter Seven

A sleeping child was a precious sight.

After a harried Gabe left, Brooke pulled a chair beside A.J.'s bed to watch him sleep. He lay on his back, arms flopped outward, head tilted to one side. Lips parted, his breath was slow and even with the occasional deep, restful sigh. Dark lashes splashed onto baby-round cheeks that looked as soft as down. His eyelids, large for his small face, were as delicate and translucent as fairy wings. She wanted to touch them but refrained, lest he waken.

Pale moonlight filtered in through the window. Brooke could see him clearly, a necessity given the clutch of fear strangling her stomach. As long as she didn't take her eyes off him, A.J. would be safe.

The emotional day of digging through family photos followed by the bizarre phone call and the time with Gabe and A.J. had left her weary, but she refused to sleep. Instead, she focused on the threatening phone call, considering the who and why.

As kids, Great-Uncle Samuel's kin, particularly Vincent and his sister, Marsha, had considered her a "scaredy cat." She'd been easy to intimidate, easy to frighten. No doubt they thought they could scare her away from Clayton and the inheritance with a few well-placed threats. Maybe they could. If Zach or Vivienne or some of the others didn't return to Clayton soon, she might as well give up anyway. Vivienne was still making noises about staying in New York. And Zach? Well, no one ever knew for certain what Zach was thinking until he acted.

There would be no inheritance without all six of them.

Then what would she do?

She'd get a job. That's what she'd do. Like every other college graduate, she'd find work and figure out the future from there. A future that would likely not include Clayton, Colorado, although the idea of being run out of town by her own kin brought out a stubborn streak.

A.J. moaned in his sleep and flopped to one side. Brooke jerked, horrified that her mind had wandered.

He gave another restless flop and let out a sharp cry. His face twisted. Then he whimpered.

Brooke placed a hand on his chest. "Shh."

The little boy's eyes popped open, glazed with sleep and terror. He lurched upward and screamed.

Brooke lurched, too, pulse pounding in her throat, as scared as A.J. What did she know about caring for a screaming, frightened child?

"Shh. Everything's okay. Don't cry."

The cries escalated. Whether he'd had a nightmare or just awakened scared, a pat on the chest wasn't enough to soothe him.

With a prayer on her lips, Brooke pulled him to her. Chubby arms clutched at her neck and squeezed hard. Hot tears dampened her neck.

"Daddy. Daddy." The shuddering, heartbroken little voice tore at Brooke's heart. Poor little man was so upset, and she was virtually a stranger.

"Daddy will be back soon." Please Lord, send Gabe home right now! "Don't cry, precious. Don't cry."

Shuddering sobs racked A.J.'s small body. Between cries, he babbled, and Brooke despaired at not understanding his baby talk.

"Did you have a bad dream?" she crooned. Rocking back and forth, she patted his back, feeling helpless but longing to give comfort. "You're okay. You're okay. Brooke's here."

She didn't know what else to say as his cries continued, deep and heartrending. She wondered if she should call Gabe, then scoffed at herself. She *was* a scaredy cat—afraid of a crying two year old.

Shaking, her own anxiety matching the child's, she began to softly sing "Amazing Grace." It was the only song she could think of at this hour, the song her mother had sung to her.

Slowly, A.J's sobs dwindled to shudders and the grasping hands around her neck loosened. Worried he'd scream again if she stopped, she continued to sing, thankful that the melody and her voice soothed him. Singing was a small thing, but the sound seemed to be the thing A.J. needed at the moment.

The power of that knowledge filled her with new courage. She had something this child needed, a simple thing called a woman's love and attention.

With the warm, sleepy, little-boy scent of Gabe's son strong in her nose, and his need for her even stronger, Brooke made a terrifying decision.

She was going to take that nanny job. She was going to be here for A.J. and Gabe.

Please God, she prayed, don't let me fail.

She met him at the front door.

Silhouetted in the golden light between the

porch and living room, a sleepy smile on her face, Brooke welcomed Gabe home.

It was a strange thing to feel welcomed by the babysitter as if she belonged there and he was the head of the house coming home after a long day's work. The sight warmed a cold place inside him.

"Is everything all right?" she asked, voice low and husky with fatigue.

"For now." Tired and bewildered himself, Gabe let his frustration come through in the two words.

"I was about to make some cocoa." She plucked at his sleeve. "Come in and tell me what happened."

The warmth spread from that cold spot into his chest and through his tired limbs. "The little guy do okay?"

She'd started to walk away but now she paused, expression uncertain. "He had a nightmare. I didn't know what to do. I'm sorry, Gabe."

"For what?" He hitched one shoulder. "Kids have bad dreams. Is he asleep now?"

"Yes. I rocked him."

"That's what I do."

"It is?" she asked.

He nodded once. "I'll look in on him."

"He's okay… I promise. I didn't leave him for a minute until just now when I heard you drive up." Her blue eyes were wide and worried.

A frisson of alarm tingled his nerve endings. "Did something else happen?"

"He cried. He called for you. I was afraid—"

"Hey." He touched her. She was smaller than he'd noticed before, coming only to his shoulders. "You wouldn't be here if I hadn't trusted you to watch him."

He turned down the hall toward A.J.'s room, found his son sleeping in the moonlight, covers kicked to the end in a wad. Brooke had drawn a chair up beside the bed and he could envision her sitting there the entire time he'd been gone. He hadn't worried about A.J. once during the time he'd been at the mine, a rare occurrence for a man who hadn't trusted his son's own mother. Gabe pulled the jungle-print quilt up to A.J.'s neck and turned back toward the kitchen.

He found Brooke waiting for him again in the hall, hands clasped as though she'd been wringing them in worry. "Is everything all right? Was he okay?"

"He's fine, Brooke. Stop worrying. He's sleeping like a baby." He smiled at the description, hoping to pry a return smile from her. He wouldn't mind seeing that dimple again just now.

Brooke gave a brief nod and pivoted toward the kitchen. He followed, puzzled by her anxiety while also mindful of the pleasant differences in the way a female and male walked. Her tangled mess of hair swayed against her back. The oversize college sweatshirt hung to mid-thigh over a pair of black leggings.

Eyes forward, Wesson.

"Packs of instant in the upper cabinet," he said, more to break his train of thought than to give orders.

"I know." She tossed a smile over her shoulder and took down the red and white box. "I hope you don't mind. I looked. The crime spree continues."

He chuckled, feeling less tired by the minute. "Yesterday the silver. Today the cocoa."

"Marshmallows?" She hoisted the opened package.

"Might as well live dangerously."

The dimple flared. "Sugar rush at one in the morning. We won't sleep at all."

"I probably won't sleep much anyway. But I apologize for keeping you out so late."

She scoffed. "I just graduated college. Late is my normal."

"Oh, right." *Thanks for the reminder.* Some of his energy dissipated. He slid wearily onto the high-backed chair and rested his elbows on the table. "I don't know how to thank you for being here tonight. Name your price."

Busy poking numbers on the microwave, her back to him, she stiffened. "Don't insult me. I came over as a friendly neighbor. This is what small-town people do for each other." The microwave whirred into action. She turned to face him, hands white-knuckled on the counter at her back. "But I do need a job."

He perked up. "Meaning?"

"I've decided to be A.J.'s nanny. That is, if you still want me."

Gabe was sure his mouth dropped. She'd been adamant. "What changed your mind?"

"A.J. You." She shrugged. "I don't know. Maybe I shouldn't…"

"Oh, no, you don't. No backing out now. You're hired." He'd talked to a dozen people about Brooke Clayton, including the pastor. They'd all agreed she was honorable, trustworthy and a solid human being he could trust with his child. He'd already figured that out on his own. "Can you start tomorrow?"

"I—" Her eyes were wide as if she were looking for a reason to say no. "What time?"

"I'll need to be at the mine fairly early. Eight at the latest. After tonight, I want everything checked thoroughly. Every piece of equipment, every vent, everything."

The microwave beeped. She popped the door open and removed the two mugs, setting them on the table. The sweet scent of chocolate curled into the space between them. Brooke scooted her chair close to the table and reached for the marshmallow package.

"Okay." Simple as that, A.J. had a caregiver he adored. The pressure lifting off Gabe was immense. "What happened out there tonight?" she asked.

Considering he'd never sat across the kitchen table from a woman at one o'clock in the morning to share his concerns about work, Gabe wasn't sure where to start. When had anyone been willing to listen at that hour?

Never. Until now. A near stranger, who didn't feel like a stranger, wanted to know and seemed genuinely interested.

So he told her. And she listened.

He wasn't sure what to do with the feelings churning beneath his rib cage. What exactly was he feeling? Warmth. Comfort. A sense of homecoming, which made no sense, all things considered. Yet, there it was, whirling around inside him, bewildering and wonderful.

Many times in the past he'd arrived home late from work or travel. A man who ran a corporation worked long hours. Too keyed up to sleep, he'd sat alone, flipping through channels or prowling the downstairs like some nocturnal creature. He hadn't minded. Not really. He wasn't selfish enough to expect anyone to get out of a warm bed for his sake.

Maybe that's why calling Brooke tonight had been so difficult. He didn't like asking anyone for favors. Yet, Brooke was still here long after she could have returned to the comfort of her bed, commiserating and trying to help him resolve the issue. And she'd agreed, astonishingly, to be A.J.'s regular caregiver.

A man could get used to this kind of attention. She was not only good to look at, she was a nice woman.

Hands cradled around a cup of instant hot chocolate, Brooke leaned toward him. Long, blond waves swung forward, kissing the side of her face, drawing attention to her full, curving lips. "What made the police think someone was in the mine?"

Glad for something to do besides stare at Brooke, he dropped another handful of marshmallows into the steaming drink and stirred. "The 9-1-1 caller heard voices."

A small frown puckered her eyebrows. "Why would a caller be at the mine at this hour? You don't run night shifts. No one should have been there at all."

He pointed his spoon. "My question exactly. The 9-1-1 caller was the likely culprit."

"Well, the pump didn't turn itself off, and you said it wasn't malfunctioning. Could one of the workers have accidentally flipped the switch before leaving this afternoon?"

"Before I can answer that, I'll have to question everyone tomorrow." He popped a mini marshmallow into his mouth, savoring the burst of sugar on his tongue.

"Will the flooding do any damage?" The plastic package crinkled as Brooke, too, reached for a marshmallow.

"The engineers will have to check. One thing's for sure—water in the shafts will set us back again." First, the breakdown with the ventilation system and now with the pump. His corporation was too safety conscious for him to believe the equipment failures were coincidence. "I'm thankful no one was inside. Under the right conditions, without that pump activated, a mine can flood in a hurry."

She poked at her marshmallows with a spoon, swirling them in a circle. "That's a scary thought."

"Tell me about it. I'm starting to think someone is intentionally sabotaging us."

"Why?"

He lifted the cup, sipped. The melted sweet stuck to his lip. Brooke laughed and handed him a napkin. "It's better in your mouth than on it."

"Thanks, Mom." He licked his lips, then dabbed them with the napkin. "A few people don't want the mine reopened, most notably a group of environmentalists that don't live in Clayton and don't understand what we're trying to do here. They've sent ugly emails."

"Clayton is none of their business."

"Won't get any argument from me, but they're threatening a legal battle."

She arched a brow. "Can they do that?"

"My attorney isn't worried. He says they can harass and slow things down but they can't win. Taking care of the environment is something Emmanuel Corporation is proud of. I intend to keep it that way."

"I saw the handbills you've sent out all over town."

"PR in a new location helps. If locals know our corporation wants to put into the community as much as we take out, they're more likely to be on board with the changes."

"You're a smart businessman. If Clayton is to survive, we need an industry here. The town should be thanking you, not getting in the way." She drained her cup and sat it on the table with a soft click. "I should go."

"Yeah." He pushed his own mug aside and stood. "The earlier I start in the morning, the earlier I can quit. I have a church meeting tomorrow afternoon."

"At Clayton Christian?" When he nodded, she went on. "That's my church. Or it used to be when

I lived here. My cousin Arabella mentioned the new Care Committee meeting. She wants me to get involved."

"You should. Tell you what—why don't I knock off at the mine and pick you and A.J. up at one? We'll grab lunch and head over to the meeting." A warning in the back of his head told him to hush, but the energy pulsing through his veins increased with every word. She was a Christian. Same church. Same interests in the Care Committee. No reason not to share a ride. And a lunch.

Brooke didn't answer immediately and he thought she might turn him down. She carried both mugs to the sink.

"Leave them," he said.

"I'll clean them up in the morning. Okay?"

"I don't expect housekeeping."

She smiled. "I like to stay busy."

"No argument from me then. You can take A.J. over to your place, too, if you have things to do there."

"Okay." She headed toward the back door.

Gabe flipped on the porch light. He shouldn't insist. He should let the subject drop, but he wasn't asking her for a date. Not exactly. She was just the babysitter. "So, about tomorrow—"

She flipped her hair off her shoulder, bottom lip caught between her teeth. As though the answer cost her something, she said, "We'll be ready."

His chest filled with pleasure, a pleasure way out of proportion to something as simple as a ride to church. At his age, he should know better than to push the envelope.

She stepped out onto the patio. Golden light shot through her blond hair and turned it to a halo around a sweet face. "Good night, Gabe."

"Thanks, again, Brooke. I don't know what I'd have done without you tonight."

She shrugged. "You've managed."

True, but she'd made his life so much easier. "I'll walk you over."

She glanced toward the dark space between their houses. "No need."

"Did you find your key?"

"No, but I found out who took it." Her hands slid into the pouch of her sweatshirt. "Chilly out here."

She was right, but he wasn't letting her change the subject. He'd been convinced she'd lost that key. "Who?"

"The same people who called me this afternoon and told me to get out of town."

Gabe stepped out on the porch with her. If she was in danger...

He glanced around the quiet, sparsely populated neighborhood. They were the only two houses on this section. The light and the subsequent shadows disappeared quickly beyond the porch, eaten

up by the darkness, leaving only moonlight to il-
luminate the fifty yards between their back doors.
"Was that what scared you this afternoon?"

She nodded. "I wasn't expecting it. She spooked
me."

"She who?"

"I'm not sure exactly, only in general. Someone
from my great-uncle Samuel's side of the family."
At his raised eyebrows, she enumerated. "Vincent,
his sister, Marsha, and her beer-guzzling husband,
Billy Dean, my cousin Les. Anyone or all of my
great-uncle Samuel's side of the family could be
responsible. If they can frighten me enough to
leave town, they inherit my grandfather's estate."

"I don't like the sound of that."

She huffed a short, soft laugh and raised both
hands. "What? You think I can't take them down
with a karate chop?"

His mouth quivered. She was feisty and cute.
"I'm serious, Brooke. You could be in danger.
Greed can motivate some people to do any-
thing."

"They're kin. They want to scare me off, but
they won't hurt me." Something in her expression
said she wasn't really certain of that.

"Why don't you bunk over here in my guest
room? Get your locks changed before you spend
another night alone."

"Henry Johnson was supposed to have come

today, but he didn't make it. I'll be fine tonight, though. Don't worry." She stepped off the porch into the darkness. Gabe followed.

She whirled. "You shouldn't leave A.J. alone."

"He's alone right this minute, Brooke. It's a dozen steps and back, not halfway across town."

"Still. Something could happen."

He took her arm and started walking toward her back door. She kept looking over her shoulder as though expecting his house to burst into flames.

"Stop it," he said. "You're making me nervous."

"He's too little to be alone."

"No argument about that." They reached her back door and Gabe waited for her to flip on the porch light. "Mind if I come in and check things."

"No need."

"Humor me."

She did. He made a quick assay of both levels while she barricaded the front door with a chair beneath the knob. He'd never known if that actually worked, but the action gave him a measure of peace.

"If you so much as hear a creak before morning, you call me. Got it?"

"The chances of creaks are good in this old house."

He fisted both hands on his hips and offered his best CEO stare down. "Promise me, Brooke."

She saluted. "Yes, boss. Now get back over there to your baby."

Gabe exited the house and stood on the porch until he heard the lock turn and the chair slide into place. "Good night, Brooke."

Her muffled snort came through the door. "Go home, Gabe."

He loped across the lawn, dialed her cell phone and told her to turn off the porch light. He waited at the back door, watching until the house went dark. Then he flipped off his own lights but remained there in the dark, praying for her safety.

Manny would tease him if he knew about Brooke Clayton. She brought out the protector in him.

He didn't like that someone was trying to frighten her.

But he did like the fact that she'd agreed to work for him. He could keep a better eye on her that way.

Brooke Clayton lived alone. She needed him, but unlike Tara, Brooke was not the irresponsible dingbat he'd first thought her to be. He'd been wrong about that. She was smart and sweet and thoughtful, not to mention as pretty as a Rocky Mountain sunrise.

A little voice whispered in his ear. *Face it, Gabe. You're getting a thing for your neighbor. Your very young neighbor.*

With a groan, he leaned his forehead against the back door and hoped he had enough sense to keep a friendly distance.

Chapter Eight

The Clayton Christian Church fellowship hall buzzed with volunteers when Brooke arrived with A.J. on her hip and Gabe at her side. As they came through the door, heads turned. Speculative smiles flickered from Brooke to Gabe and back again. They'd had the same reaction at the Cowboy Café when they'd stopped for lunch.

Brooke didn't mind, but Gabe noticed and seemed uncomfortable. In the café, he'd pointedly told Erin, Kylie and anyone else within hearing range that Brooke was A.J.'s new nanny. She didn't know why that bothered her but it did.

Well, okay, she did know why it bothered her. She was a normal female with a normal ego, a need to be considered special by a special man. Gabe was a good-looking, successful guy. Any woman in her right mind would want to be on his A-list.

He'd been unusually quiet today, too. She'd

figured he had business issues on his mind, but when she'd asked about the Lucky Lady, his reply had been short, his attention elsewhere.

Was he regretting the decision to hire her?

She chanced a glance at his strong profile. No, it wasn't that. He'd been waiting with a cup of gourmet coffee and another word of thanks when she'd arrived at his back door this morning. He was probably tired after their late night. She certainly was.

Arabella, smile wide, came toward them, her triplets in tow. After exchanging pleasantries, Gabe took A.J. and moved off toward Reverend West and a clutch of men gathered around the coffee pot.

"So you agreed to be A.J.'s nanny?"

"I still can't believe it." She'd hardly slept last night thinking about being alone with a child every day for hours on end. Even though this morning had gone well, she'd been a nervous wreck for the four hours Gabe had been gone.

Arabella hugged her. "Good. He'll keep you busy." She pumped an eyebrow. "Hanging out with his handsome, single dad will be icing on the cake."

"He's really sweet."

"The child or the dad?"

Brooke smiled. "Both actually. Gabe walked

me home last night and wouldn't leave until I was safe and sound."

"Wow…what a guy!"

"Arabella, will you stop? It's not what you think." She told her cousin about the phone call and the missing house key.

Frowning, Arabella shoved a lock of thick hair away from her face. "That's spooky."

"Tell me about it. A house feels really empty when you're alone and someone else has your key."

"Did you call the sheriff?"

"Vincent told me to my face that he wanted me out of town. I'm sure he or Marsha or someone in that family is responsible. With Uncle Pauley as mayor, what police officer is going to take me seriously?"

Arabella placed slim fingers on her forearm. "You're welcome to stay with us."

"You have your hands full enough. Besides I have my new job and Gabe right next door. I'll be okay." The words were brave, but anxiety knotted beneath her breastbone. What if Gabe was right? What if someone was willing to do her harm to gain Grandpa George's inheritance?

A shiver snaked down her spine but before she could dwell on the worry, Reverend West, a large, forty-something man with toffee-colored hair, called the group to order.

"Thank you for coming, all of you. The Lord has to be pleased at such a large group who's willing to donate time and effort for the good of others. The Bible tells us in Matthew chapter twenty-five that anything we do for those less fortunate is the same as doing it for Jesus. I like thinking about that, don't you?" A wide, warm smile lit the preacher's brown eyes as he looked over the gathered volunteers. Across the room, people nodded or smiled in response.

A good feeling filled Brooke in a way she hadn't felt in a long time. She was glad she'd come. Maybe she could volunteer for the help hotline or to clean the church. She wouldn't mind doing grocery shopping for the elderly either as long as A.J. could go along.

She looked around to see the little boy playing with a group of children, including Arabella's triplets and a chubby blond girl of grade-school age. Jasmine Turner was with them, doling out some of Arabella's oatmeal cookies. Brooke relaxed, comfortable that A.J. was safely in the care of someone else for a while.

When she returned her attention to the pastor, the volunteers were breaking into groups.

"What are we doing?" she murmured to the woman beside her.

"Committees." Pen in hand, the woman tapped a notebook, though her blue eyes studied Brooke intensely. "Do you have a preference? By the way, I'm Darlene Perry, the church secretary."

The name and face were familiar and Brooke sorted through her memory to place the woman. Darlene hadn't been the pastor's secretary five years ago, but she was definitely a local. When the name clicked, pity stirred in Brooke. Darlene Perry had once been a very pretty woman. Now she looked too frail and fragile to hold a job. Complexion pasty-gray, her dark blond hair, though neatly curved around her thin face, had no sheen, and her eyes were dull, lines radiating from the edges as though she worried a lot. Brooke suspected the woman wasn't well.

"I'm Brooke Clayton."

Darlene's gaze pierced her. "I know."

In Colorado Springs Brooke would have found the reply odd, but not in Clayton. Here, the Clayton kids were known by all, thanks to Grandpa George and his brother, but neither she nor her siblings had always been happy about the notoriety.

A.J. came toddling across the concrete floor in her direction, his face lit from within. Brooke's happy meter rose. He was such a great little boy. She swung him into her arms, listening to the responding gurgle of laughter as he pressed his cheek to hers.

"You should volunteer for the church nursery," Darlene said. "They always need help."

"Me? No. Not interested." Brooke was already shaking her head. Her insides shook, too. No way she'd put herself in that position. Taking care of A.J. was scary enough.

"Well, that's too bad. Gabe's little boy sure seems to like you." The frail woman shifted, looked away and then back again. "I was wondering…" She paused for a deep breath. Before she could go on, Gabe rejoined them.

"You were about to say?" Brooke encouraged, curious.

Darlene's thin lips pressed together. Her gaze slid to one side. "Excuse me. I think the phone is ringing."

As she hurried off toward the church office, Gabe stared after her. "What was that all about?"

"I don't know. She seemed kind of nervous about something, didn't she?"

"Don't tell me Darlene's another relative of yours."

"If you mean one of Uncle Samuel's clan, no. I don't really know her that well, but I think she may have been a friend of my Aunt Katrina." Brooke bit her bottom lip, trying to remember *something*. "Anyway, she and Aunt Kat are about the same age. She lives in a pretty little house on the edge of town, but she's always kind of stayed to herself. I don't remember seeing her at church before." But then, she'd been gone for a long time. A number of new people now attended the church her grand-mother had built.

"Do you see that little girl over there? The one with the long, blond hair and glasses?" Gabe motioned to the older child she'd noticed earlier playing with the triplets. When Reverend West saw the direction of their gaze, he approached the girl and said something. The child looked up and smiled their way, then ducked her head shyly. After a pat to the child's shoulder, the reverend started across the room toward Brooke and Gabe.

"Who is she?"

"Darlene's daughter, Macy. Reverend West asked me to serve as a big brother of sorts."

"Are you going to?"

"I'm considering it. From what I'm told, Darlene doesn't have any relatives, and Macy is shy with people, especially men. I guess she's never known her father."

The stray memory niggled at Brooke's brain again. She could almost hear her mother and Aunt Lisette discussing something about Darlene and her baby. What was it? "That's nice of you. Kids, even girls, need a male role model."

"That's what the reverend here tells me. Better watch him, though. He's pretty good at persuading."

As beefy as a linebacker, face naturally jolly, the pastor clapped Gabe on the shoulder and picked up the conversation. "That I am. So, are you persuaded yet?" He glanced at his watch. "I've given you ten whole minutes to think about my idea." He chuckled, letting the joke soak in. "You'd be doing a good thing, Gabe. Darlene's had some health issues, and after working here all day, she doesn't have the energy for anything extra."

"Who cares for Macy while Darlene's working?" Brooke asked.

"Oh, that's one of the perks of working for the pastor." He tapped his chest. "Soft touch, my wife says. Darlene brings Macy with her. Little thing isn't a bit of trouble. She watches TV, reads or plays her video games."

Brooke thought any day she couldn't be outside or working out was wasted. "What does she do for exercise? Sitting around that much can't be healthy."

"Couldn't agree more," the pastor said. "That's why I'm determined to find someone to get her out more. Not just her, but any of these kids who have single, working mothers. Darlene's a special case because she's my secretary but also because of her health. She isn't physically up to extracurriculars."

"Okay," Gabe said. "I don't know how much time I'll have, but you've convinced me of the need."

Reverend West pumped Gabe's hand. "Whatever

you can do. An hour a week, an afternoon, anything at all. The Lord will bless you."

"I have some free time today. Maybe we could take Macy with A.J. to the park this afternoon and get acquainted. I'll have to wrangle Brooke's help, if that's all right."

"Funny you should say that. Darlene specifically asked about Brooke. She said she'd like for Macy to get to know you." He shot a look toward the open church office door. Darlene sat at a reception desk, speaking into the telephone.

Brooke blinked in surprise. She barely knew the older woman. "She did?"

"Probably because you're active and athletic. Macy's too young not to be getting some fresh air and exercise every day." Reverend patted his belly. "Can't have her be a couch potato like the preacher."

Macy was already out of shape. For a fitness buff like Brooke, the need to see the child moving around more started a buzz in the back of her brain. As long as Gabe was with them…

"He's right, Brooke," Gabe said. "You'd be a terrific influence on Macy. You told me yourself you're bothered by the lack of fitness opportunities in Clayton."

Brooke pinched her bottom lip, thinking. She'd also told him her impossible heart's desire—to work with kids. Was that where he was headed with this line of thought? "I think you may be as good at persuading people as the pastor."

"Got another idea for you, Brooke," Reverend West said. "Let me run this past you. The church has talked about starting a rec program for our area youth, but we never had enough adult interest."

"It's a real need," Gabe said. "I see kids roaming around town, doing nothing every day. They're bored and we know what happens with bored kids."

"Exactly. An outreach ministry of this type could touch lives in a powerful way."

Brooke loved the idea. As a teenager, she'd wished for something more to do in this tiny community. What she didn't love was the fact that Reverend West apparently wanted her in a leadership role. "What do you have in mind?"

"Whatever we can make work. Maybe a church sports team or exercise classes, something to draw kids' interest and bring them in. I don't know for sure. That's why I need someone like you to put an idea together for us."

"Me?" Her pulse kicked up.

"From what Arabella tells me, you've always been into sports. Didn't you run a marathon recently?"

"Half-marathon." Which had nearly done her in, but she'd finished. "I like to run and I play lots of sports and do some dance, but that doesn't qualify me for something like this."

"Sure it does. Interest is everything. You know what you enjoy, what's required to stay fit, and you're young and in great shape yourself. Kids respond to that. You're the natural person to start a program."

"I don't know…" He was scaring her to pieces. No way could she take on the responsibility of a roomful of kids.

The pastor leveled his wide smile at her. "Pray about it?"

Not that her prayers did all that much good, but… "Well—okay, sure. I guess."

"Great. You won't be sorry."

As she watched the pastor head toward the office to share the news with Darlene, Brooke hoped he was right.

Chapter Nine

Gabe figured he'd regret the time he wasn't spending at the mine, but lately work didn't seem as important. He hired good people. The mine had a manager and any number of experts. They could handle the day-to-day operations with the same efficiency his employees handled his other business enterprises around the state. He had a cell phone. If there was problem, they'd call him.

A.J.'s high-pitched squeal of laughter echoed across the town square, a pretty park area located right in the center of Clayton. Brooke's laugh followed A.J.'s.

Gabe retrieved the Frisbee that Macy had thrown over his head and jogged back to the threesome. Twice this week he'd skipped work to hang out with Darlene Perry's ten-year-old daughter. Anyway, she was the excuse he used. That A.J. and Brooke tagged along was only natural.

Brooke. He saw his nanny every day and the time didn't seem to be enough. His belly flip-flopped. The signs were all there. Attraction. Compatibility. Respect. *Disaster*.

Eyes dancing, Brooke thrust out a hand. "Give me that Frisbee. Let me show you how it's done."

He puffed out a breath. "You throw it, you chase it."

"If you can't take the heat, big boy, stay out of the kitchen."

Gabe fisted one hand on his hip, eyes narrowed. "Is that a challenge?"

Her fisted hand mocked him. "Are you wimping out on us?"

"Give me that Frisbee." He reached.

She yanked it back, lips twitching. "No, you don't. I'm throwing. You're the receivers. You, Macy and this little puppy right here." She reached down to tickle A.J. under the chin. He threw his arms around her legs, nearly toppling her. She caught herself and him just in time. "Ready, A.J.? Chase Daddy and Macy."

"We're ready, too, aren't we, Macy?" Gabe asked. "See if you can beat me to the catch."

Macy pushed at her plastic glasses and offered him a shy smile. A sweet kid, she didn't quite know what to do with a rowdy male and his son, but she seemed to enjoy their outings. He'd taken her for a snow cone the day of their first trip to the park, not that she needed the junk food as Brooke was quick to remind him, but the time together was a way to get better acquainted. Brooke and A.J. had gone along, naturally. It made no sense to take one without the other two, and having A.J. and Brooke along broke the ice with the little girl. Macy interacted well with A.J., was kind and gentle even when he'd spilled purple snow cone on her pink shoes. That alone had scored big points with Gabe.

He could tell Macy had spent about as much time with a man as she had in physical activity. Pretty much zero. He, however, had grown up with younger sisters.

"You'll beat me," she said.

"Only one way to find out." He got down in a runner's crouch. "Come on, A.J. We're gonna race."

Brooke held the flying disc high over her head, arm back in pitching formation. "On your mark."

Macy squeaked but went to a crouch in imitation of Gabe. He winked at her, and her smile was radiant.

"Get set."

A.J. saw the two of them in a racer's stance and tried to do likewise. Macy giggled.

"Go!"

The trio streaked off, Gabe holding back to an

easy lope. A.J.'s short legs churned the green grass. His arms pumped madly. Macy took the lead as Gabe jogged alongside his son.

"Run, little buddy. Beat Daddy."

"Here it comes, you guys," Brooke yelled.

Gabe glanced over his shoulder to see the Frisbee release from Brooke's hands. Whistling overhead, the disc flew past him toward Macy.

"Macy, turn around!"

She whirled. Behind the plastic glasses, her blue eyes widened. In reflexive defense, both hands came up to protect her head. The Frisbee thumped against her palms and bounced to the grass.

A.J. rushed to catch up. "I get it."

By now, Gabe was next to Macy. He bent to retrieve the plastic disc and handed it to the little girl. "Sorry, A.J., Macy got that one. Nice stop, Mace."

"I almost caught it," she breathed, eyes still wide with surprise.

"Sure did. Next time, close your fingers and the catch is yours."

"I almost caught it. I never caught anything before."

They fell in step and headed back toward Brooke, who came jogging toward them. The woman had more energy than a hive of honeybees. Dressed in white shorts and a hot pink T-shirt, blond hair flying around like wings, she hadn't even broken a sweat. He, however, felt the dampness bleeding through his T-shirt.

He dropped a hand to Macy's shoulder. "Do you play any sports at school?"

She shook her head. "I stink at sports."

"Hey, cut that out. You're talking about a friend of mine."

She cocked her head and gave him a puzzled smile. "Oh."

"You keep working out with Brooke and me, and you'll be as fast as Brooke."

"I want to look like Brooke." Macy gazed adoringly toward the athletic blonde jogging toward them. "She's so pretty."

Gabe couldn't argue that, though Brooke's looks were only a small part of why he couldn't get her out of his thoughts.

He tilted his head to study the serious little girl. "You know, you kind of do."

By now, Brooke had reached them. "What's that?"

"The two of you. You sort of resemble each other."

"You think?" Brooke studied the ten year old with mild interest, and then with good humor said, "Blond, blue eyes." She clapped her hands together once. "There you go. We're twinkies!"

Delighted, Macy grinned. "Yes, we're twinkies. I wish I was pretty like you."

From Brooke's expression, the painful comment pricked her heart in the same way it touched his. No little girl of ten should have low self-esteem.

"You are pretty, Macy. Remember, we're twinkies?"

"Oh, yeah." A tiny smile lifted the corner of her mouth but didn't light her eyes. They had their work cut out for them to help Macy feel good about herself.

"You both have a dimple, too. Right there." Gabe poked his finger gently into Macy's cheek and winked. "Come on. A.J.'s headed for the climbing toy without us."

Brooke sucked in a worried gasp and bolted toward A.J. Gabe and Macy followed at a slower pace. He didn't get why Brooke freaked out if A.J. so much as moved without her moving, too. But in the end, he knew his son was in good hands.

When A.J. saw her coming, he shrieked with laughter and took off running, certain they were playing a game. She caught him, swooped him high over her head and spun him in a circle. His laugh echoed straight into Gabe's heart.

"A.J. likes Brooke, too," Macy said quietly. "She's really nice."

Gabe watched his son with the nanny, throat constricting. A.J. did like Brooke. In the space of such a short time, he'd bonded with her. Last night his son had cried when she left for the day. Cried and asked for "Book, Book." Gabe had fought like mad not to call her back and ask her to stay for dinner.

His son needed a mother.

Gabe's gaze focused on Brooke as she followed A.J. up the slide, held him between her knees and came sailing down, arms overhead like a kid on a roller coaster.

With a shake of his head, he dropped his gaze to the patch of green grass.

Yes, his son needed a mother.

But not Brooke Clayton.

The chat and clatter inside the Cowboy Café swelled to a pleasant din as Brooke dashed inside, arms chilled and wet from the sudden cloudburst. She shook the droplets from her hair and stood on the mat someone had placed by the door. She felt at loose ends today, a surprise given her reluctance to work for Gabe in the first place. He and A.J. had driven up to Denver to visit family and take care of some business. He hadn't invited her along and it was silly to feel left out. She'd had to give herself a talking to after his Hummer had pulled out of the garage this morning. She was only the nanny.

Somehow she felt like more. Clearly, A.J. returned the feelings. His daddy didn't.

She adored the child and the man had her thinking romantic thoughts.

With a shiver, she brushed the raindrops from her arms and sniffed the scents of fresh pot roast and sweet, yeasty bread, nearly moaning with enjoyment.

Calls of "Hey, Brooke," and "How you doin'?" joined a half dozen head nods to acknowledge her entrance. She returned the greetings, the warmth of the café chasing away the afternoon chill. She'd missed this, missed the familiarity of knowing and being known. Though she hadn't realized it until now, she'd missed the comfort of being surrounded by friends and neighbors whose grandparents and grandkids she knew. Her damp spirits lifted.

The tables were full, so Brooke settled at the counter, her favorite spot anyway. The *Denver Post* at her elbow headlined the Colorado Rockies' win over the Mets.

Kylie Jones plopped a vinyl-covered menu on the counter in front of her. "The Rockies are doing well this year. Have you been to a game?"

"Not this year." Not in several years. She'd been so intent on Marty and his plan to go to the mission field that she'd lost focus of the things *she* cared about. What had she been doing with Marty in the first place? Except for their shared faith, they were nothing alike. His idea of physical activity was surfing channels with the remote control. Not only had she not been in love with Marty, she'd not even enjoyed his company that much. What kind of woman decided to marry a man solely because he couldn't have children? But that's what she'd done. When Marty confessed his inability to father a child, she'd considered him an answer to her prayers. The pressure to have kids was off.

Stunned by the realization, she flipped open the menu. "What's the special? Roast beef?"

Kylie grinned. "Smells good, doesn't it? Roast beef with red potatoes and green beans loaded with bacon bits."

Brooke's eyes rolled to the back of her head in mock ecstasy. "Perfect. After that, I'll have an excuse to run five miles in the rain."

"When did you ever need an excuse?" Kylie propped her elbows on the counter and leaned forward. "I heard you're starting a youth program for the community."

Brooke's pulse jumped. "Where did you hear that?"

Kylie lifted a shoulder. "Here and there. You know how Clayton is. If you think too hard, we'll hear you in the café. So, are you or not? It's a great idea. The school would probably let you use the gym. You could have a summer league for basketball and baseball or maybe you could organize hiking and rock climbing groups." She took a breath. "How about tennis? And in the winter, you could teach kids to ski and snowboard."

"Whoa, Kylie." Brooke held up a hand. "I told Reverend West I'd give the idea some thought. That's all."

"Oh." Kylie wilted. "Too bad. Everyone has been so excited about it."

"There's that much talk already?"

"What else are we going to talk about in Clayton? Well, except the mine. Vincent said there have been some problems and they may have to shut down."

Trying not to react to the mention of her troublesome cousin, Brooke said, "Shut down? That's the first I've heard of anything that serious."

"Well, you should know, being close to Gabe Wesson." She gave Brooke's shoulder a little push. "He's a babe, isn't he?"

"Yeah, I guess he is." There was no guessing to it. He *was* a babe, as Kylie put it, and she missed him. She was pathetic. Gabe left town for one day and she couldn't stop watching the road for his Hummer. "So, what about you and Vincent? I hear there's a wedding on the horizon?"

She hated to bring up the subject of Vincent, but she and Kylie had once been friends. Only a year apart in age, they'd played ball together, shared secrets, braided each other's hair and mooned over the same rock singers. Sad how time and distance could separate people. Sadder still to see a nice girl like Kylie end up with Vincent. She prayed he was different with his fiancée than with the rest of the female population, but she doubted he was. Vincent's pretty-boy looks and smarmy charm fooled people outside the family.

"Order up, Kylie," a voice called.

"Be right back." She zipped away.

During her absence, Brooke fed the old-fashioned jukebox and chatted with Deanna Stutz, proprietor of the town's one and only beauty parlor, Hair Today.

"How's your manicure holding up?" Deanna reached for Brooke's hand.

"Pretty well, considering the abuse it takes. That was such a great day." The afternoon she, Jasmine and Arabella had spent in Deanna's shop had created a fast bond among the three women. Brooke wasn't sure if they'd made any inroads on Jasmine's relationship with Cade Clayton, but she'd opened up a dialogue with the younger woman. The result was a budding friendship she enjoyed.

"Your finger's looking better." Deanna pressed the slightly crooked, now unsplinted, knuckle on Brooke's pinky finger.

"Doesn't hurt at all anymore."

"Good. You girls come back soon. We've got some new colors for summer that would look terrific with sandals. Manicure, pedicure, facial, the works." Deanna winked. "For all three of you, I'll make a package deal."

"Sounds great, Deanna." As soon as she saved up enough money again. "There's my lunch. Talk to you later."

She returned to her seat just as Kylie deposited the steaming plate. She groaned appreciatively. "The cook is a genius."

"Can't argue that." Kylie tilted her chin toward the order window. The large, ruddy face of Gerald Hicks grinned out at Brooke. She wiggled her fingers in greeting and gave a thumbs up.

Erin had hit the jackpot the day she'd hired Gerald and Jerome Hicks to run the kitchen. Where Gerald was round and easygoing, Jerome was skinny and fastidious, a true odd-couple set of brothers who created pure culinary delight for the folks of Clayton. The Hicks brothers may not have Cordon Bleu credentials like Vivienne, but they understood small town taste buds.

When Gerald's jolly face disappeared, Kylie lingered to talk.

"Give me the scoop," Brooke said. "When's the wedding? What are your colors? What's the dress like?"

A cloud passed over Kylie's face but was quickly replaced by a smile, making Brooke wonder if she'd imagined the reaction because of her negative feelings toward Vincent. She hoped so. She wanted her old friend to be happy.

"I'm doing the wedding myself," Kylie said. "You won't believe this, but I've gotten pretty good at planning budget weddings. I've helped several of the girls in town and they all seemed really pleased."

Brooke saluted her friend a forkful of roast. "Not surprised at all. Remember how you use to cut pictures out of bride's magazines and arrange them into scenes?"

"I still do!"

They both laughed. Brooke was glad she'd stopped into the café and taken the time to visit with Kylie. She was still a great girl. What she saw in Vincent, however, remained a mystery to Brooke.

From behind her, Brooke heard the bell jingle over the opening door. Cool air swirled in. The change in Kylie was dramatic. Her smile disappeared. Her eyes grew wary. She pushed back from the counter and in a guilty whisper said, "I should get busy."

Brooke figured the change could only mean one thing. Vincent had walked in and caught his fiancé talking to "the enemy" side of the family. Brooke rotated on the counter stool enough to see the new customer. It wasn't Vincent, but Vincent's sister, Marsha Harris, stood inside the doorway, umbrella dripping on the floor, icy gaze going from Kylie to Brooke.

Brooke lifted a hand in greeting. "Hi, Marsha. Wet outside, isn't it?"

The steely glare would rival a laser. Brooke's sumptuous roast lost its flavor. She sighed. Being at odds with anyone was not her nature.

Marsha snapped the umbrella shut and hung it on the coat tree next to the door before coming toward Brooke with a determined air. Thin, with the temper to go with her red hair, Marsha could make her presence felt. Brooke braced herself.

Without preliminary, her cousin leaned close and murmured, keeping her voice low, tight and controlled, though anger boiled beneath the surface. The strong odor of cigarette smoke spoiled the pleasant scent of lunch.

"You have a lot of nerve."

Brooke carefully put her fork down. Having a sharp instrument in hand right now might not be wise. "More than I used to. You'd be smart to remember that. I'm not the same easily intimidated girl you remember."

"Don't make trouble for my brother."

"I don't know what you're talking about."

"You told Gabe Wesson that Vincent was causing the problems at the mine."

Not exactly true but Brooke didn't argue. Marsha had a way of twisting things to suit herself.

Marsha's shrill voice rose. "You hate my brother and me just the way your grandpa hated mine and stole everything from our family."

The cheerful chatter inside the small café ceased. Heads turned, listening. A deep flush heated Brooke's face. Her stomach knotted.

"This is not the place to air your grievances against my family, Marsha," she said quietly.

"Leave my brother and me alone." Marsha jabbed a finger close to Brooke's nose. "Or sleeping with Gabe Wesson won't be enough to protect you."

With one final, furious glare at Kylie, Marsha whirled and stomped out of the café.

Face flaming, hands shaking, Brooke fought back humiliated tears. She wanted to run away and hide. She wanted to crawl under one of the tables and curl into the fetal position.

She wanted a big strong shoulder to cry on. Gabe's.

Maybe she wasn't so brave after all.

Chapter Ten

"Don't you pay one bit of attention to her." Jerome Hicks had appeared from the kitchen, nostrils flaring and flapping a dish towel in the direction of Marsha's wake as if shooing flies. "If you were stuck with Billy Dean Harris for a husband you'd be bitter, too. The louse hasn't worked in so long he's crippled his fingers from crushing beer cans all day."

She offered him a weak smile. "Thanks, Jerome."

Awkwardly, he patted her shoulder. "You're welcome. Now, clean that plate like a good girl and I'll bring you one of Arabella's cherry-cheese tarts—on me."

Gerald's jolly red face poked out the order window. "Better take him up on that, Brooke. Last time he sprung for dessert was 1972."

Brooke pushed back from the counter. "That's kind of you, Jerome, but I should go."

God bless them, they were trying to cheer her up. But she had to get away before the tears came.

Jerome harrumphed. "Nonsense. You are not going to let Marsha Harris cheat you out of lunch and dessert. Kylie, bring Brooke a tart. Extra whipped cream."

"Really, I can't."

Kylie did as she was told but slid the saucer onto the counter with eyes averted. "Sorry," she whispered and then hurried off to wait on other customers. Marsha's untimely appearance had taken the sunshine out of the waitress.

Brooke wondered again why a nice girl like Kylie would fall for a jerk like Vincent, but she didn't ask. Jerome was a gossip of the first order. Even though he was kind enough to cheer her up with a cherry-cheese tart, he wouldn't hesitate to tell everyone he knew about the unfortunate incident. Including the last bit about Brooke and Gabe.

Worst, Deanna still lingered over her meatloaf and mashed potatoes. The woman's radar was always up and in the receiving mode.

"I hope you won't repeat what Marsha said."

Jerome's eyes gleamed brightly. "Concerning you and the handsome Mr. Wesson?"

"I'm his nanny and his neighbor. That's all."

He patted the back of her hand. "Got it. Now eat that tart."

The flow of conversation and noise in the café had begun again. Jerome disappeared around the counter and left her alone and not at all certain he would keep the incident quiet. If they'd heard, and they most assuredly had, she knew the rest of the establishment wouldn't. The sound of Deanna's boisterous voice made that a definite. Everyone in the beauty shop would have the word before dark.

Poor Gabe. He'd be horrified. A Christian man running a company and trying to win approval in a small town did not need rumors of an illicit affair with his son's nanny.

Guilt crawled over her skin like a black widow spider. Why did Marsha have to drag a fine person like Gabe into their family squabbles?

Brooke's hand shook as she cut into the dessert. Even the sweet, freshly whipped cream wasn't enough to take the sour taste out of her mouth.

She felt the stares burning into her back, the hum of interest buzzing around the room. A voracious hunger for gossip fueled small towns. She and Gabe would be the latest hot topic.

With an apologetic glance toward the kitchen, she paid for the meal and left the diner.

Despite the rain that followed him over the mountains and forced him to drive with the top up on his 1966 Mustang, Gabe was feeling good.

He'd had such a terrific day in Denver, he'd opted to leave the Hummer and show off a little in the Mustang. He'd visited family, bought an apartment building and scored four box seats to watch the Rockies trounce the Dodgers. Somehow he knew Brooke would enjoy the outside boxes right on top of the action more than Emmanuel Corporation's high-rise suite. The outing would be great for Macy, too.

Ever since he'd agreed to play big brother to the ten year old, he'd been having fun coming up with ways to draw her out and get her laughing. Her shy smile appeared more often now that she'd gotten to know him better. Part of that he credited to Brooke. She made a terrific big sister for the little girl, instinctively knowing what Macy needed, just as she did with A.J.

Her statement that she didn't want kids still perplexed him. Frankly, he didn't buy it, and from her overreaction when A.J. bumped his head or got out of her sight, he wondered what had happened to make her so fearful.

Easing the slick classic car into his usual parking spot, he jumped out and trotted toward Brooke's front porch without even stopping off at his own place. He couldn't wait to tell her about his plans for tomorrow night. She was gonna love them.

The minute she opened the front door, he knew something was wrong.

"You've been crying," he accused.

She swiped an oversize sweater sleeve across her eyes. "I'm okay."

"Right." She didn't look okay. He glanced past her into the living room. The furniture covers were gone, the room cleaned and smelling of lemon cleaner. "Did you get another phone call? Someone else harassing you?"

"No. Not exactly." She looked over his shoulder, frowning toward the car. He'd expected her to get all bubbly when she saw the Mustang, to get excited and want a ride. "Where's A.J.?"

"At his grandma's house."

"I missed him. I hope he has fun."

He wanted to ask if she'd missed him, too. He'd certainly missed her. One day without her sunny presence and he couldn't get her out of his head.

"I feel weird without him, too, but he's gone only for tonight. Grandma and the aunties needed some A.J. time. I'm going back to Denver tomorrow." He reached into his hip pocket. "Got us all some tickets to the ball game. Me, you, Macy and A.J."

"Oh."

Again, he'd expected excitement. She loved the Rockies. Instead, her "oh" sounded like distress.

A dozen thoughts shifted rapidly through his mental file system. She didn't want to go with him.

She didn't want to be A.J.'s nanny anymore. She wanted him to get lost and not come back.

His good mood was fading fast.

All day, while he'd met with Manny and then the board of directors and during a client lunch, his mind had wandered to Clayton, and A.J.'s nanny. Manny had noticed his distraction, but he'd blamed the continuing issues at the mine. That was part of the problem. The other part was standing in front of him with a red nose and puffy eyes.

He'd prayed about her on the way back from Denver. Prayed and ask the Lord to give him platonic feelings for the nanny. By the time he'd pulled into the yard he'd decided to treat Brooke Clayton as a kid sister. A kid sister who was helping him mentor a ten-year-old girl. The idea made perfectly good sense. No mother wanted to let her little girl go off to ball games and parks with a single man. Having Brooke along solved any issues of impropriety.

This evening, though, his Lancelot gene kicked in. Something was wrong and he needed to fix it. "Want to come over for steaks?"

"I had a big lunch."

"So come for the company. I want to run some ideas past you."

A flame of interest sparked in her blue eyes, flickered and went out. She shook her head, blond hair catching the lights from room behind her. "I don't think so, Gabe. Maybe we shouldn't be seen together without A.J. or Macy."

Gabe went very still. "What does that mean?"

She turned away from the door and went into the living room. He followed, examining the stab of hurt her comment had given him. She didn't want to be seen with him?

"What's going on, Brooke? Talk to me. I thought we were friends." *Yes, there you go. Friends. Brother and sister. Neighbors.*

"This afternoon my cousin Marsha announced to the Cowboy Café that you and I are more than friends." The expression on her face was pained, embarrassed.

"You mean, as in dating?" A bizarre, unbidden flame sparked in his chest. Dating? He and Brooke? Just as quickly the flame went out. From the look on Brooke's face, the thought of dating a man his age was downright humiliating.

"No, as in—" Her gaze slid away from his. Red heat colored her cheeks.

Realization struck Gabe right between the eyes, harder than a falling boulder. She was talking about way more than dating. "As in an affair?"

Lips pressed tight, she nodded.

Anger stirred his blood. Someone had humiliated her because of him. "That's why you've been crying, isn't it?"

"I never meant drag to you into my family problems. You've worked hard to develop a good reputation in Clayton, but people love to believe the worst. This kind of thing, in a town this size, will hurt your business. Not to mention cause a lot of embarrassment. I'm so sorry."

"That's why you're upset?"

She nodded again. "I like you too much to muddy your name because of the Clayton family's dislike for each other. It's wrong to hurt you and A.J. because of me."

The sick feeling in Gabe's gut disappeared. She wasn't blaming him. She was trying to protect him.

"Who would believe a pretty college girl like you would look twice at a guy my age?"

Her mouth dropped. She tilted her head, bewildered. "What a silly thing to say. Age has nothing to do anything. You're a fantastic man. Any girl with brains would be interested."

She was serious. Did that mean *she* was interested?

Lord, help him.

The tightness in his throat loosened. With a soft murmur he hoped sounded like comfort, he enveloped Brooke in his arms and pulled her to his chest.

She fit perfectly.

He didn't give a whit about gossip and rumors.

Seeing Brooke upset over them, though, bothered him royal.

Stroking the soft hair he'd longed to touch, he rocked her back and forth as he would A.J. His mental alarm warned him that this was not A.J. and that the feelings rattling around in his chest were not paternal. Nor brotherly.

She was too young. He was too old. What would people think?

She'd claimed age didn't matter, but she'd not walked in his shoes with Tara.

When she shuddered once and burrowed closer, he shut the alarm off and savored the moment to enjoy a beautiful woman in his arms. Not any woman. Brooke Clayton. A few seconds and then a few minutes passed and yet he held her, reluctant to break the mood.

She liked him too much.

He closed his eyes, remembering another time and place, another woman. He'd vowed never again to let his feelings for a woman steal his common sense.

Slowly, surely, and with the strength of will that had forged a corporation, he loosened his embrace and set her away from him.

He liked her too much, too.

Long after Gabe left, Brooke stewed over the events of the day. He'd behaved strangely about

Marsha's ugly remarks, but those minutes in his arms had just about done her in. She'd wanted him to kiss her and when he'd made that silly statement about their age difference, she'd been sorely tempted to kiss him first.

What planet was he from anyway? No one worried about age these days, at least not an age difference of a few years. Well, maybe he was close to ten years older, but the years were not a big deal.

She was washing her face when the light bulb of realization flared. She stared into the mirror and blinked. Maybe Gabe was trying, in his nice way, to let her know that he was not interested in her as a woman. She was his nanny. Maybe he was using the age thing as an excuse to keep her at arm's length.

She made a face at the mirror. "Shut up. You think too much."

After dragging a brush over her head, she pulled her hair back with a pink headband and returned to the cleaning frenzy she'd gone on while she cried like a big baby over Marsha's hateful remarks. After all the years of being bullied by her cousins, she should be strong enough to let their words slide off like rain on plastic. So far, not.

This was one of the many reasons she'd never wanted to live in Clayton again. The memories o

Lucy and the tensions with the other side of the family zapped her joy.

According to Arabella, the Bible said to pray for those who despitefully use you. Was it possible to be sincere in a prayer like that? Arabella meant every word, she was sure, but Arabella was a gentle soul who would never hold a grudge.

"Lord," she said honestly. "I'd rather see Uncle Samuel's clan move to Siberia, but if You say I should pray for them, I will. And I'll try to mean it." She thought hard, attempting to come up with an honest prayer. Finally, it hit her. "Please help my Uncle Samuel's side of the family find peace and love on the inside. If they feel better about themselves, maybe they'll be nicer. Amen."

Granted, the prayer was a weird one but God knew what she was thinking. The next year in Clayton would be much easier if Marsha and Vincent became nicer people.

With a couple of hours left before bedtime, she turned on a CD and went back to cleaning. Other than Arabella's general upkeep, no one had touched the house since Mom died. Brooke had been the only one still at home at the time. Zach and Vivienne had been long gone and uninterested in anything related to Clayton. They'd come home for the funeral and left just as quickly. But if either of them returned to fulfill the conditions of

Grandpa George's will, they'd need a decent place to stay.

"It'll take months to sort through all this," she muttered. What if neither sibling returned? She'd heard little from either since the reading of the will.

Fishing her cell phone from her pocket, she scrolled to Zach's number and pushed send. When her brother's strong voice came on the line, she slid down next to the bed and leaned her back against the side. A dusty scent rose from the mattress.

"What's up, Gigglebot?"

"Hi, Lump." The childhood nicknames curled warm and nostalgic inside her. A smile curved Brooke's lips. "I just wanted to talk, to see how you are."

"I'm good." Brooke knew those two words were about all she'd get out of Zach on that topic. If his right arm was hanging by a thread, he'd claim to be all right. "Staying busy."

"When are you coming home?"

"Don't know yet. I'm working on it. How are things on the home front?"

She told him about the reopening of the mine and the nanny position.

"Way to go, sis. I'm proud of you." Zach knew her anxiety around kids. "So how's the job going?"

"A.J., that's the little boy I'm babysitting, is

adorable. I love him. But," she said wryly, "his dad had no clue who he was hiring or he wouldn't have."

"Hey. Don't do that. Don't." Zach used his iron-cop voice.

Brooke swallowed. "What if something happens?"

"What if it doesn't?"

She had no argument there. "He's so precious, Zach. I'm already crazy about him. Today, Gabe— that's his dad—took him to Denver and I missed them both so much. After avoiding kids all my life, this feels weird."

"Good weird?"

"Yes. No." She shoved a hand through her hair. "I don't know. To make matters crazier, Reverend West is trying to convince me to start an athletic program for the town's youth." She laughed softly. "Can you imagine me doing such a thing?"

"Sure can. You're a natural."

"Don't you start, too. It's almost like God is forcing me to be with kids since I've come back here." She told him about Macy. "Her mother is the church secretary, Darlene Perry."

"I remember her. Lived in that pretty little house on the edge of town all alone. Just her and the baby."

"Arabella mentioned the gossip about them. People wondered who Macy's father was, but

Darlene stayed to herself most of the time. It's odd that she's suddenly insisting I spend time with her daughter. Gabe signed on to be her big brother of sorts but Darlene specifically asked for me to play big sister."

"Why you?" he asked.

"I don't know. As I said, it's kind of odd."

"Gotta agree. Be careful."

Brooke chuckled at the flare of her big brother's protective instincts. "Darlene Perry is as frail as a dandelion. She has health problems, though I'm not sure exactly what's wrong. She seems to be a nice, gentle woman. Anyway, the pastor thinks so. I have nothing to fear on that front." She took a breath. "Gabe thinks Darlene picked me because I'm athletic and Macy needs to move around more. He even said we look alike. Blonde, blue eyes, one big dimple."

"Maybe she's a long-lost Clayton."

They both laughed at the silly notion. "Grandpa George was a scoundrel but I can't see that happening, can you?"

"Not and live to tell about it," Zach said. "Grandma had her standards."

"Since we're on the subject of Grandpa, have you heard anything at all from Lucas? Arabella was fretting over him yesterday. She's tried to reach him by phone. No luck."

"Not a word."

"His boss in Georgia, or rather his former boss, told Mei he'd seemed distracted by something and then one day he just got up and announced he was going to Florida."

Zach sucked in a surprise. "Here?"

"That's what I heard. Since then, he's pretty much disappeared. No one, not even Mei or their mom can reach him."

"Lucas can be a wild child, but that doesn't sound like him." Brooke could practically see the frown gathered between Zach's eyes. "Not where Mei and Aunt Lisette are concerned."

"Exactly. We thought you might do some checking. See if you can locate him. His mom is pretty worried. And if we don't find him, none of us is going to inherit that money. I feel greedy saying that, but Arabella especially needs it. You know how she is. She won't complain, but things are tight for her and the kids."

"I may be out of communication myself for a while, but when I have a chance, I'll see what I can do," Zack promised.

"You're not involved in anything dangerous, are you?"

He snorted. "Brooke, I'm a cop."

"How reassuring," she said dryly. "Take care of yourself, okay? I love you."

"Ten-four on that one, Gigglebot."

Brooke was about to ask him directly if and

when he was coming home when a noise drew her attention. She turned toward the sound coming somewhere from the front of the house. "Hold on a second, Zach. I hear something."

"What kind of something?"

"I think someone's at the front door."

"This time of night?"

"It's probably Gabe."

"The next-door neighbor? Do you trust this guy?"

"Implicitly. He's wonderful and almost as protective as you. I like him a lot, Zach."

"Sounds like a guy I should beat up. I'll stay on the line."

Brooke giggled. "You're so funny. Bye, Zach. I love you."

"Wait a minute—"

Chuckling, Brooke clicked the End button and used the mattress as leverage to push up from the floor. Dust circled around her face. She coughed, waved away the dancing particles and headed toward the living room.

The few minutes of conversation with her brother had bolstered her in a way little else could. Seven years older, Zach had been her protector, her friend, her hero. When the tragedy with Lucy had happened, fifteen-year-old Zach had been the only one who'd said it wasn't her fault. He'd also been the one to sit on the edge of her bed and soothe away the nightmares that had plagued her for years.

Someday she'd like to marry a man as awesome as her brother.

Her thoughts went instantly to her next-door neighbor. The noise from the outside came again, a thump and a knock. With thoughts that Gabe waited, Brooke slid the phone into her back pocket and hurried.

She stepped into the living room…and screamed.

The front door was wide open…and a dark, hooded figure loomed on the porch.

Chapter Eleven

Gabe heard a scream. The hair tingled on the back of his neck.

He shoved up from the lawn chair, alert and listening. Nothing.

Had he heard an animal in the distant woods? He searched the tree line for illuminated eyes or movement. Nothing.

His cell phone chirped.

"Gabe. Come over. Hurry."

The fear in Brooke's voice told him where the scream had originated.

"I'm coming." He bolted toward her house, crossing the fifty yards in a gallop. She let him in immediately. "What's wrong?"

"Someone tried to get in." She wrapped her arms around her body, trembling like a leaf in a windstorm. Her lips quivered. "A man, I think. In dark clothes and a hood"

"Did you see his face?"

"No. When I screamed, he ran. I slammed the door and locked it, then I called you."

"You opened the door to him?"

"The door was open. I know I closed it after you left earlier, but it was open. Wide open." Hysteria edged her words. Bright blue eyes were wide and frightened. "Gabe, my door was open and he was right there." She pointed at the space just outside the door on the porch.

"I'm calling the sheriff." He punched in the numbers he'd added to his contacts after the trouble at the mine, then wrapped one arm around her shivering shoulders. Someone was going to pay for scaring her like this.

As soon as he'd been assured an officer was on the way, he pulled Brooke down on the couch and drew her into his arms. She was scared. A big brother would hold his sister if she was scared.

She buried her face in his neck and clung to him. "How did you get here so fast? Oh, I'm so glad you did."

"I was on the back patio." Not that he was ready to share, but he'd been praying for guidance about her. "I heard you scream."

"Thank God."

Grimly, Gabe agreed. Maybe God had kept him outside for this very purpose. Brooke needed him. The protector in him rose both furious and determined. Gently, he tried to calm her down. He talked about the tickets to the Rockies and shared his idea of buying some sporting equipment for the church. "With your input, of course."

She responded thinly, saying little, but gradually the violent shudders eased.

By the time the sheriff arrived and pulled the squad car into the driveway without use of flashing lights or siren, Brooke was mocking herself for being frightened.

He was glad she was feeling better, but a hooded man on the porch was not a laughing matter.

He met Sheriff Diggers at the door and apprised him of the incident. Brooke filled in the details.

The older man removed his cap and scratched his head. "Lot of nonsense going on around here lately. Ever since you decided to reopen the Lucky Lady."

Gabe looked sharply at the lawman. "You think this has something to do with me?"

"Can't say. Not yet anyway." He replaced the cap. "You folks sit tight while I have a look around outside."

"I'm going with you."

The sheriff's keen gaze took his measure. "Got a flashlight?"

Gabe turned to Brooke, eyebrows raised in question. She nodded. "In the kitchen. I'll get it. I'm going, too."

He didn't argue. After what she'd experienced, the need for human companionship would be strong. He took her hand, felt the soft skin and delicate bones and got mad all over again. Brooke didn't deserve this kind of hassle. He'd be madder still if the incident had anything to do with him.

"I'm going on," Diggers said. "Come when you want. Be careful. I don't figure anyone's still around but we have to consider he might be."

The sheriff's heavy boot steps clomped out the door. Gabe and Brooke went for the flashlight. By the time they found a battery with enough juice to run the light, Sheriff Digger's voice hollered at them.

"You folks come on out here. I want to show you something."

"This will do." Gabe flipped on the weak light and led the way outside. "Where are you?"

Sheriff Diggers answered, "Round on the east side of the house. Watch your step. There's some junk over here. Blame near broke my neck on some kind of planter."

Beside him, Brooke stifled a nervous giggle. "Sorry."

"Your caller left you a message. Don't make sense to me. Might to you."

Holding tight to Brooke's hand, Gabe followed

the faint glow of flashlight to where the sheriff waited, wreathed in shadows.

"A message? What kind of message?" Brooke asked.

The lawman shone his light on the side of the house. Bright red paint oozed down the white siding. One single word gleamed like fresh blood: *Lucy.*

Brooke sucked in an anguished gasped. Slapping a hand to her mouth, she whirled and ran.

"You want to tell me what this is all about?"

Gabe's face, grim with fatigue and stress, loomed over her. He'd paced the hardwood flooring of her living room for the past five minutes, one hand to his hip, the other rubbing the back of his neck, stopping periodically to fire off a question.

Brooke had no intention of dragging up her worst memory for anyone, especially Gabe. The sudden appearance of her sister's name had shaken her more than the hooded man. To her relief, Sheriff Diggers didn't seem to remember a child's death that had occurred years ago. "The sheriff will talk to Vincent. I'm sure he's responsible. He or his sister."

After snapping photos and asking a few questions, Sheriff Diggers had driven away. Brooke wasn't at all certain he'd say a thing to Vincent considering he and Pauley Clayton, Vincent's dad, played dominoes together. With his retirement less than a month away, the sheriff had his own reasons for not upsetting old friends.

"I know you don't get along with your cousins, Brooke, but you're starting to sound paranoid. You said yourself the man didn't have Vincent's build. Maybe the sheriff was on to something when he asked about your friends in Colorado Springs."

She bit down on her bottom lip. The hooded man had been tall and lanky. Vincent was muscle-bound.

"Why would anyone from college follow me to Clayton to scare me?"

He pinned her with a stare. "You tell me. Didn't you break up with a boyfriend not long ago?"

"Well, yes, but Marty?" She made a scoffing noise. "He's going to be a missionary."

"Some guys go off the deep end, Christian or not, when their plans are thwarted."

"Not Marty," she insisted.

"Who did the breaking up? You or him?"

Brooke gnawed at her bottom lip, thinking of that awful day of the breakup and the broken finger. Marty had said such mean things to her about Lucy. She sucked in a quick breath. Oh, my goodness. Marty knew about Lucy.

"The breakup was mutual. Sort of." She stared

toward the closed and locked door. Marty was tall and lanky.

No, no. It didn't make sense.

"You broke the guy's heart, embarrassed him in front of his buddies and now he's stalking you."

"I'm not the kind of girl that drives men off the deep end." The idea of Marty as a stalker didn't compute.

"You should consider the possibility. At least tell the sheriff so he can check into Marty's whereabouts tonight."

The only people who bore her any animosity were her own flesh and blood. She knew Marty. He would never do such a thing. He had plans, goals, dreams.

And she'd shot most of them down with the breakup.

She pressed a shaky hand to her forehead. One thought kept returning. Marty knew about Lucy. He knew about Brooke's part in her sister's death. He knew Lucy was her breaking point. And in the end, he'd mocked her fear of having children. He'd changed his stand against parenting and had expected her to go along with his decision. When she hadn't, he'd been furious.

Maybe she hadn't known him as well as she'd thought.

Too exhausted from the emotions of the day to

argue, she bounced steepled fingers against her lips. "You're right. I'll call the sheriff tomorrow."

She'd phone Zach, too. He'd be more interested in answers than the local sheriff. Though a decent enough man, Linden Diggers was set to retire and preferred his domino games and coffee at the Cowboy Café to investigating crimes.

"Good." Gabe rubbed the back of his neck again. Fatigue sharpened the lines around his eyes.

Regretful for keeping him up until the wee hours when he'd traveled far and worked hard today with more on the agenda for tomorrow, Brooke said, "Thank you for coming over tonight, Gabe. Everything is locked up tight and we both need some rest." Like she would actually sleep after this. "You don't have to stay any longer. I'll be fine."

He glared at her, incredulous. "You think I'm leaving you here alone after what happened? No possibility. You can stay with me tonight, in the guest room."

"And add fuel to the rumors?" She started to shake her head, then thought better of it. A pounding had started in her temples.

He stopped again, dark eyes searching hers. "Call Arabella. Stay with her. I'll drive you over."

"No. She'll be asleep. And you should be, too. Someone wanted only to upset me, Gabe. If he'd wanted to hurt me, he could have." She shivered, stunned by that ugly truth. "I'm not afraid to be here alone the rest of the night." Regardless of Gabe's questions about Marty, Brooke was convinced she knew the source of her tormenters. "My cousins want me to leave town. If I show fear now, they'll think they're winning and try something else."

"What if it's not your cousins?"

"It is."

He sighed, unmoved by her stubborn stance. "If you won't stay at my place, I'm staying here."

Did the man not understand the power of gossip in a small town?

"I'll call Jasmine and ask her to come over for the night. How's that?" She wasn't sure why Jasmine's name popped into her head, but since their spa day, they'd gotten closer. Maybe she wouldn't mind.

Gabe handed her his phone. "Do it."

With a tired sigh, she pressed the numbers, relieved when Jasmine answered on the first ring. Teenagers kept later hours than a mother of triplets.

After hearing of the situation, Jasmine gasped, "Are you all right?"

"Yes, but I'd rather not be alone until the sheriff talks to Vincent."

"Oh, Brooke, I'm sorry. I wish Cade's side of the family..." Her voice trailed off. Given who his grandfather was, the mention of Cade Clayton wasn't appropriate right now. "I'll be there in ten minutes. Okay?"

Brooke hung up and returned the phone to Gabe. "Now you can go home and get some rest."

Gabe pocketed the cell. "Trying to get rid of me?"

He'd been wonderful tonight. "Not even close. But you're exhausted, Gabe. I see it in your eyes. You have enough on your plate without adding a crazy neighbor."

He crouched in front of her and took her hands in his. "None of this is your fault. I admit I thought you were a little scatterbrained at first—locking yourself out of the house and all—but what happened here tonight is real."

"You have your own problems at the Lucky Lady." She frowned, remembering something. "I forgot to tell you earlier. Kylie Jones heard you're closing the mine. Is that true?"

Looking surprised, he said, "Not at all. I wonder where that rumor got started?"

"Something about the dangerous incidents. The mine was unsafe."

Brow furrowed, Gabe studied the backs of her hands. "That's not good news. If people in town view the mine as unsafe, we'll have more staffing woes, more grief from the environmentalists."

"The rumor mill thrives on bad news or scintillating stories."

He looked up. "Such as our lurid affair?"

"You're taking this a lot more calmly than I did," she said.

The sparkle in his eyes and quirk of his lip said he was teasing. "A man might consider it a compliment that a beautiful woman would find him that alluring."

She pulled her hands away and whacked his arm. "I don't do affairs."

"That makes two of us." He pulled her hands back to him, the twinkling eyes growing a shade darker. "But I am a man, and you are attractive."

"Gabe." Her pulse kicked up. Minutes ago she was exhausted and sad. Now her blood hummed. "I—"

He touched her bottom lip with one finger. "Shh. Don't say anything sweet or I might give in to the temptation I've been fighting all evening."

Brooke was not a child. She knew what she was doing and what she wanted. She wanted Gabe to forget his self-control and kiss her.

She wrapped her hand around that one finger balanced on her lip. Softly, she asked, "What temptation?"

His palms, hard and rough from work but gentle as velvet, found the side of her face and drew her closer. "I was afraid for you tonight. Scared out of my mind. If someone hurt you…"

Brooke's heart raced. Absorbing the sensations

of his nearness, her lips curved in invitation. He sighed and moved closer. His warm breath sent a shiver along the sensitive skin. "I knew you were trouble the minute I saw you hanging from that window."

Brooke laughed softly. "Why don't you stop talking and kiss me?"

He blinked. "Bad idea."

But he kissed her anyway.

A bright light went off inside Brooke's chest. The heat and tenderness of Gabe's kiss flooded her senses. He smelled good, like the mountain forest and a clear stream. She reveled in his touch, fully aware she was falling and wasn't the least bit sorry. He kissed her once and then shifted to draw her into his arms and kiss her again.

The knock at the front door made them both jump.

Bemused and wishing she hadn't phoned a friend, Brooke pushed gently at Gabe's chest. "Jasmine."

Gabe groaned, tapped his forehead to hers and let her go. When she rose, he rose with her, squeezed her hand and went to the door.

Jasmine entered. "Oh, I didn't know you had company."

"Gabe stayed with me until you arrived."

"That's what neighbors are for." His eyes

twinkled but he took his cue and stepped onto the porch. "I'll go. If you need anything, call."

Brooke stood in the doorway. "I will."

His eyes held hers. "Lock the door behind me."

She touched his arm, reluctant to see him go. "Okay."

He lingered, searching her face for another beat before he turned and started through the darkness.

Brooke wanted to follow him, to enjoy one more kiss, to ask exactly what the kisses had meant. Instead, she shut the door and secured the bolt, then turned to her friend waiting just inside.

"Are you two—?" Jasmine sat her overnight bag on the couch and took a long look at Brooke before a knowing smile bloomed. "Oh, yeah, you are. Ain't love grand?"

They stayed up much too late talking about the hooded man and the trouble with Vincent and Marsha, but mostly they'd talked about men. Two in particular, Gabe and Cade. Jasmine was in love with a young man from the wrong side of the family and she knew Arabella did not approve.

Early the next morning, after less than three hours' sleep, Jasmine asked Brooke for help.

"I have a favor to ask." Jasmine leaned on the speckled Formica counter in Brooke's kitchen, waiting for the tea kettle to whistle on the old white porcelain cookstove.

"One good turn deserves another." Toast popped up, releasing a hot scent. "Butter and cinnamon?"

Jasmine shook her head as she extended a saucer. "I'm a jelly girl."

Gingerly juggling the hot bread, Brooke dropped a slice on the saucer and went to work on her own. "What kind of favor?"

Jasmine's hesitation gave her fair warning. She was not going to enjoy this favor.

"Go with me this morning to talk to Arabella."

"About what?"

"Cade and me," she murmured softly.

"Oh."

Jasmine rushed on. "You know how Arabella feels about us being together."

"She has good reasons, Jasmine, even though you're the most mature and sensible eighteen year old I've ever known."

"Age is not the only reason she opposes our relationship, Brooke. Admit it. You're prejudice against him, too, because of his family." She sighed. "But Cade's not like them. He's sweet and honest, and he loves and respects me."

Brooke chomped down on her toast. "What do you want me to do? Tell Arabella to lighten up? She loves you, Jas. She only wants the best for you."

"I know. She's been wonderful. I love her like a big sister and I hate to hurt her...but I love Cade. I won't give him up."

"Has she asked you to?"

Jasmine looped a lock of hair behind one ear. She took a deep breath and said, "You know what it's like to be young and in love. Don't deny it. I saw the way you looked at Gabe."

Still digesting the events of last night, Brooke was not ready to discuss her feelings for Gabe Wesson. "What does that have to do with talking to Arabella?"

"I want you there to make things easier for me, for her, for all of us. Kind of a family council. She's going to need someone to talk to afterward."

Brooke didn't like the sound of that. "So what's to talk about?"

"Cade is coming over to the house this morning. We're going to tell her the news."

Alarm prickled Brooke's scalp. Arabella would die if Jasmine was pregnant. "What news?"

"Cade and I are getting married."

Chapter Twelve

The scene in the vaulted living room of Clayton House was tense to say the least. Brooke, who kept wondering how she'd gotten involved in the first place, was glad Arabella had confined the triplets to the playroom with a DVD. This council of family, small as it was, throbbed with conflict.

To his credit, Cade Clayton behaved like a real man. He sat beside Jasmine on Grandma's silk rose divan holding Jasmine's hand while he laid his hopes and dreams before Arabella.

"We want your blessing, Arabella. It's important to both of us. I promise to take good care of her."

Arabella, wringing her hands like a tragic Shakespearean heroine, paced the faded Turkish rug in front of the hearth. "How do you propose to live? You're nineteen, Cade. Jasmine is eighteen. Neither of you have any real job skills, no college degrees."

Cade's jaw tightened. "I have a job and we will both go to college. You have my word on that."

"Why can't you wait until you *finish* college?"

"Cade wants to be a doctor, Arabella." Jasmine's eyes were bright with unshed tears. Apparently, this was harder than she'd hoped. "That takes years."

"My point exactly. Years. How will you support yourselves if Cade goes to medical school? The cost is in the hundreds of thousands, and he'll have to study hard. He can't hold a job and attend medical school."

Cade's mouth set in a stubborn line. "We'll manage. I'm not afraid of hard work."

"I know you have good intentions now, Cade, and I respect that, but you're too young to realize how hard it is to get started in life. If you get married now, chances are, you'll never finish college, much less medical school." Arabella's voice filled with emotion. "Look around me. I married at nineteen, had three babies. As much as I love my girls and enjoy my work, I have no other choices. I don't have an education. I'm living in someone else's house. God has taken care of me, but life has not been easy."

"We don't expect easy, Arabella. But Cade loves me," Jasmine said with quiet insistence. "He'll be there for me. I'll be there for him. We won't abandon each other when the going gets tough. Together, with our faith, we'll be happy."

Brooke was sure the kind-hearted Jasmine had not intended the words as a stab, but Arabella looked stricken. When life had proved hard, her husband had abandoned her and the triplets.

"I hope you're right." The doubt in Arabella's voice hung in the air like a miasma.

With a sigh, Cade rose and drew Jasmine up with him. "I'm going to marry her, Arabella, and I'm going to love her and take care of her for the rest of our lives. If you won't give your blessing, I hope you'll give us your prayers."

With that final, eloquent speech that said volumes about the young man's maturity, he took his leave.

With a pleading gaze over one shoulder, Jasmine looked from Arabella to Brooke and back again, then followed her fiancé out the door. Brooke got the message. As much as she loved Cade, Jasmine loved Arabella, too. Expecting the conversation to end in this manner, she'd requested Brooke's company so that Arabella would not be alone when she and Cade departed.

When the door clicked shut, Arabella collapsed heavily onto the vacated couch. "What am I going to do?"

Brooke went to her, sitting close. "There is nothing you can do, Arabella. They're both of age."

"I barely know him." She studied the backs of her hands. "He's my cousin, and all I know is that Jasmine loves him and he's from the wrong side of the family."

Bitterly, Brooke thought of all the mean things Cade's family had done. "How could she let herself get involved with him in the first place? Didn't you warn her?"

"I tried." Arabella pushed at the long, dark hair falling over one shoulder. "And failed miserably, as you can see."

"Maybe Jasmine was right. Maybe we object more to who Cade is than how old they are."

"Their ages and lack of education are a huge factor, but of course I object to who he is. Don't you?"

Brooke had to admit she did. "After last night, I don't want anything to do with any of Cade's side of the family. Ever."

She and Jasmine had told Arabella about the hooded visitor.

"Well, unless we can convince Jasmine to wait, I'm going to be spending more time with Uncle Samuel's clan than I ever dreamed."

Brooke put an arm around her cousin's shoulder. "This has to break your heart."

"It does, but mostly, I'm afraid for her. For her future. With no birth family to rely on, she has a long, difficult road ahead." Arabella dragged both hands over her face, blew out a deep breath and sat up straighter. With a determined set to her jaw, she said, "Enough of me fretting over Jasmine. I need a distraction. Talk to me about what happened last night. Are you sure the creepy visitor was Vincent?"

"I'm sure it *wasn't* Vincent. The man in the hood was tall and slender. But Vincent could have hired someone. Or it could have been any of the others on his side of the family. They all want Grandpa's money."

"True, but no one's bothered me at all," Arabella said. "Why would scare tactics be aimed only at you?"

"You sound like Gabe. He thinks a stalker followed me from college."

Arabella blinked, the furrows between her eyebrows deepening. "Maybe he's on to something. Things like that do happen, you know. Old boyfriends or guys who wanted to date you but couldn't. What about your ex?"

Brooke shook her head. "I gave Marty's name to the sheriff but I can't see him as stalker. The answer rests with Vincent, I'm confident, but proving it is another thing."

"Especially with Uncle Pauley as mayor."

"Exactly."

"Instead of improving relations, Grandpa George made everything worse with that will,"

Arabella said. "Some days I just want to let them have it all."

"Money can't buy nice. I just wish Zach and Lucas and the others would hurry and come home. With them here, running me out of town becomes a moot point."

"What if they don't come? I have to admit I'm concerned they won't. Not one of them has even hinted at a return since we talked at the funeral."

"Zach says he's trying. I talked to him last night before my unwanted visitor arrived." Brooke's blue eyes filled with concern. "Lucas is the cousin that worries me. No one has seen or heard from him in weeks. Meanwhile, Vincent and Marsha know if they succeed in scaring me away, it won't matter who else comes back for the year. We all have to be here to inherit."

"But you and I know something Vincent and Marsha don't. You're not the same scared little girl you used to be."

"Sometimes I wonder. Last night terrified me, Arabella."

Arabella squeezed her hand. "But you stayed. You didn't run."

"Thanks to Gabe and Jasmine."

"Stop selling yourself short," her cousin chided. "Look at how you're helping that little girl of

Darlene Perry's and the way you took on the nanny job, even though you were scared."

"I still am most of the time."

"But you're doing it. And loving the experience from what I've seen. Where is A.J. anyway?"

Brooke told her about the toddler's visit with his grandmother. "We're going up tonight to get him."

"We? As in you and Gabe?" Arabella made a small humming noise. "What's going on with the two of you? Don't say nothing. I know better."

"I'm A.J.'s caregiver—end of story." After last night, the oft-repeated phrase didn't feel true anymore. Apparently, Arabella thought the same.

"Oh, please. Give me a break. For days, every other word out of your mouth is Gabe this, Gabe that. There's more going on between the two of you than a nanny–boss relationship."

Brooke blew a lock of hair away from her face. "He kissed me last night. Or maybe I kissed him."

Arabella arched her eyebrows. "You *are* getting brave."

"I thought maybe he kissed me as a comfort thing after the scare, but—well, it wasn't a brotherly kiss by anyone's measure."

"Oh, wow. Brooke, that's wonderful." She patted Brooke's knee in excitement. "Well, come on. Tell me. How was it?"

"Beautiful. Tender. Passionate but restrained. No one has ever made me feel that special and protected." Brooke touched her fingertips to her lips. "I think about him all the time. I want to be with him. When he leaves, the room feels empty. Am I going crazy?"

Arabella clapped her hands once and laughed. "You're not crazy, honey. You're in love."

Brooke pressed a hand to each warm cheek. She'd felt nothing like this for Marty. Nothing. "Yes. Maybe. Is it possible? I don't know if I'm ready for this."

"What about Gabe? Does he know? What did he say? This is just delicious news."

Brooke's joy bubble burst. "He regretted it. He even said kissing me was a bad idea."

"Why?" Arabella looked perplexed. "You're both single. You're both Christians and you're both fantastic people."

"He thinks he's too old and I'm too young."

"Get out of here!"

"It's true. Maybe I'm not right for him anyway, all things considered. He has a son. Being the nanny is one thing, but what if I were with A.J. all the time?"

"What if?"

"You know what I mean, Arabella." A lump

rose to her throat. "I can't live with another loss like that."

"Nothing is going to happen. Lucy's death was a tragic accident. You're so overdiligent with A.J. the child can't breathe without you getting giddy from his carbon dioxide."

Brooke grinned a little at the silly, but mostly true, analogy. "Caring for a toddler is a big responsibility."

Arabella widened her eyes. "Tell me about it! Try potty training three at a time."

Brooke chuckled, then glanced at the clock over the fireplace mantle, a lovely antique piece Grandma Clayton's mother had brought from Switzerland. "I should get moving. I have a playdate with Macy in a bit."

"And I need to check on the girls. They've been quiet way too long." She cast a motherly eye toward the stairs. "Before you go, I want to ask about Macy's mother. I saw her yesterday in town. She's really ill, isn't she?"

"I think so. She puts on a good face at church, but from what Macy's said Darlene sometimes hurts too much to get out of bed. She takes a lot of medications, too."

"That's awful. Poor thing. And little Macy. That sweet child must be worried."

"She is. The more we're together, the more she talks about her mom's condition. I asked what's wrong, but she couldn't remember the name. She says Darlene goes to a doctor every week."

"Reverend West put her on the special prayer list."

"I'll add her to mine." Considering the past few days, now might be a good time to start spending more time with her Lord. He'd been on the back burner for too long.

Getting up to leave, she hugged Arabella. Her cousin clung a moment too long and Brooke knew, regardless of her outer calm, she still ached over Jasmine's announcement. "Are you going to be okay? Macy and I can come back here if you need the company. Or we can call Deanna and go for another pedicure. Macy would love that."

"I wish I could, but not today. Too much work. Once I get busy, I'll be fine." Arabella offered one final, hard hug. "What about you? Are you going to be all right alone at your house? If you have a stalker—a real one instead of an annoying cousin—you could be in danger."

Brooke suppressed a shiver of foreboding. She didn't have a stalker. Her tormentor was the same bully he'd always been.

Wasn't he?

The school gym echoed with the squeak of rubber soles against wood flooring and the rhythmic bounce of a basketball.

Having finished work as early as possible, Gabe moseyed inside to watch the handful of kids doing basketball drills under Brooke's watchful eye.

He'd known she'd be here with Macy, but the other kids surprised him. They barely noticed his entrance as Brooke took the ball, demonstrated a correct chest pass and fired one toward a boy with braces. He caught the ball and shot it back to her. She nodded and said something that brought a smile to his face.

Macy spotted Gabe and waved. Brooke turned and waved, too. Then she said something to the kids and jogged toward him, leaving them to the drill.

Gabe's stomach took a nose dive. He could stand here all day and stare at Brooke Clayton. Last night's kiss was probably a mistake, but he would gladly make that mistake over and over again.

"Hi." Dressed in gray gym clothes, her hair in a bouncy ponytail and skin glistening from the workout, she put her hands on her hips and twisted her back from side to side until it popped. "How are things at the Lucky Lady?"

"Okay." He hitched his chin toward the court. "You're good with them."

"They're nice kids."

"Where did they come from?" he asked.

Brooke made a wry face. "Reverend West rides again. They were waiting with Macy when I got to the church. The junior boys class, he claimed. These are the nerdy kids who are too intimidated to go out for ball in school." She held up a hand. "Their words, not mine."

"So you're giving them a little summer workshop."

She made a noncommittal noise. "Did you bring your gym shoes?"

He glanced down at his feet. "You're kidding, right?"

She tilted her head, mocking him. "Take off your street shoes, buddy boy. We've been waiting for you."

"We'll have to leave pretty soon if we're going to make the Rockies game."

"Afraid of playing one-on-one with a girl?" Her dimple flashed.

"In a word. Yes." He sat down on the low bench and untied his shoes. "But I love a challenge."

Call him a glutton for punishment, but time with Brooke was all he thought about. Last night had made things worse. He was a man who knew better and yet, he was drawn to the woman like the proverbial moth to flame.

He bent to his toes, stretched his calves and rotated his neck and shoulders. Then he jogged onto the court and to the woman waiting with a sparkle and a challenge in her blue eyes.

Any day now she'd wake up and realize some guy her own age was better suited and more appealing.

Hopefully not today.

Top down, the scent of pine trees ruffling the wind, Gabe's convertible ate up the curving roads from Clayton to Denver. To his pleasure, Brooke and Macy had both loved the Mustang. Brooke, who'd apparently been too distracted to notice the red machine yesterday had squealed, hopped over the door and demanded a spin around the block. Of course, he'd obliged.

Now they were nearing their destination, the Rockies' ballpark, after picking up A.J. from Grandma's. In his rearview mirror, he stole a quick peek at his baby perched high in a brown car seat. Kicked back and relaxed, talking a mile a minute to no one in particular, A.J. was in his usual good mood. Gabe's heart filled. He'd missed the little man, and though A.J. loved his grandma, he'd gone wild with excitement when Gabe and Brooke walked in. Especially Brooke.

Even his mother had noticed. She'd noticed a lot more, too.

"Brooke seems like a nice girl," his mother had said, cornering him in the hallway on his way to the bathroom. "Who is she?"

"A.J.'s nanny," he'd said, reluctant to examine

exactly how much more Brooke was than hired child care.

His mother had rolled her eyes. "Gabe. You're my son. I see the gleam in your eyes when you look at her. You haven't acted this happy since—" She paused, pursed her lips and finished, "Ever."

His mother's words stayed with him all evening. He was happy since moving to Clayton, and he'd almost forgotten how to be.

Gabe glanced at Brooke. Was she the reason?

She caught him looking and grinned as she beat a rhythm on the dash in time with the music pumping from the CD player. No doubt about it, Brooke was more than a nanny. The important question was, how did *she* feel about *him?*

Slowing, he geared down and eased into the flow of traffic to the ballpark.

Buckled in beside A.J., long blond hair lifting at the sides like wings, Macy's eyes danced behind her hot pink glasses. She'd gone as ballistic as Brooke over the car and the trip to Denver. She was a sweet kid, and the better Gabe knew her, the sorrier he felt for her. With a sick mom and no dad, she hadn't had many experiences. She'd never been to a pro game, never been to the Denver zoo or the National Park, never gone skiing or hiking or much of anywhere, and she knew next to nothing about relating to a male father figure. Gabe figured he and Brooke could remedy that.

"Almost there," he called toward the backseat.

A.J. kicked his legs while Macy grinned. Beside him, Brooke yanked her Rockies ball cap from beneath the seat and slapped it on her head. "Ready to rumble."

She was so cute Gabe had a hard time concentrating.

"Did you hear from Sheriff Diggers today?" he asked.

Holding the cap in place with one hand, Brooke shot a quick look toward the children. She'd been adamant about not telling Macy about last night's incident. "Vincent had an ironclad alibi. He was working out at the Circle C with a half dozen other guys."

"They vouched for him?"

"Yes." Blue eyes gone serious, she leaned closer and dropped her voice. "I knew he wasn't the one, but I still think he's responsible."

"What about your old boyfriend?"

"I don't know. The sheriff hadn't followed up on Marty, but he said he would."

Gabe's jaw tightened. "If he doesn't, I will."

"You sound like my brother." When she'd told Zach about her late-night visitor, he'd gone quiet for a second before promising to have a word with Sheriff Diggers. Knowing Zach, he'd have a quiet, firm word with Marty and Vincent, too. "Let's not talk about that anymore, okay?"

"Right. We're out for fun. No fretting allowed." However, Gabe knew he'd go right on fretting until the guilty man was caught.

He pulled into a parking lot, paid the attendant and put the top up as the crew piled out of the Mustang. He watched Brooke with the children, marveling that a woman barely out of college could be so motherly with children not her own. When she fell in step beside him, he hoisted A.J. onto one hip and took her hand. She reached for Macy on the other side and like a normal, American family, the foursome made their way through security and into the park.

The crowd inside the stadium was already thick, but they found their seats near the field and halfway between home plate and first base.

"Gabe, these seats are amazing. How did you manage to get this close?"

"This is so cool," Macy breathed, blue eyes taking in the huge space, the green field, the giant scoreboard in center field. She lifted a disposable camera Gabe had given her and snapped away.

Their reaction pleased him. "Anything for my best girls."

He didn't know what possessed him to say such a thing and was relieved when Brooke laughed. "That's not what you said when we hammered you in basketball."

"A fluke. Nothing more. And for the record, a three-point win does not qualify as 'hammering.'"

Ball cap shading her face, Brooke exchanged looks with Macy before they both burst into giggles.

The truth was he'd worked his tail off to stay up with Brooke's speed and quickness.

"You held your own," she said. "I was pretty impressed."

Ever the kind one, Macy soothed. "The boys all thought you were cool."

"Cool, huh? I'll take cool." He patted A.J.'s swinging leg. "How about that, buddy? Your old man is cool."

"Don't let it go to your head," Brooke teased, nudging him with an elbow. With the pair of them seated shoulder to shoulder, the incidental touches were unavoidable. Whoever installed these seats was a genius.

As soon as the National Anthem ended, Brooke had them all cheering like fanatics for the home team. At the crack of the bat, she was on her feet, fist pumping the air. When the Rockies scored the first run, she started a round of high fives that spread to the fans in adjoining seats.

A baseball game had never been this much fun.

Gabe caught the enthusiasm, and when he'd whistled through his teeth, Brooke insisted he teach her and Macy the dubious skill.

"You never know when you'll need to whistle loud enough to rupture eardrums and send dogs into spasms," she'd said gleefully.

"Lofty goals," he'd answered, and then he'd demonstrated. The girls did a fair amount of air-blowing. Mostly, they giggled. The resulting care-free hilarity produced an atmosphere of pure, energetic joy.

Mom was right. He hadn't been this happy in a long time.

He slipped an arm over the back of Brooke's seat, letting his fingers graze the soft skin at her nape. She tilted her head, smiled and shifted closer. Contentment settled into Gabe's chest. Brooke Clayton made no demands. She simply gave exactly what he needed.

Halfway through the fourth inning, A.J., bored with sitting, slid from his chair to play with the toys they'd wisely brought along. A collection of plastic animals formed a zoo on the fold-down seat. Macy moved over to play, too. A.J. began to fuss.

Time for more distraction. Gabe roused himself from the pure pleasure of Brooke's nearness.

"Anyone for a deep-fried Twinkie?"

"Gabe!" Brooke whacked his forearm.

Gabe grinned and rubbed at the spot. "Just wanted to see your reaction. We'll go for the Rockie Dogs first. Twinkies later."

Her blue eyes twinkled. "You are so bad."

"I know." He patted his chest with mock pride. "So what do you say? Dogs, Twinkies, cotton candy, junk food here we come?"

"I say we're at a baseball game." She grappled on the floor for her purse. "I'll have a Rockie Dog. Loaded."

He pumped a fist in the air. "My kind of woman. Come on, kids, concession time."

Macy hopped up immediately, eager for a new adventure. A.J. ignored him in favor of a plastic zebra. Brooke moved toward the busy toddler.

At the crack of a bat, Gabe rotated toward the sound.

Brooke gasped. Before he could compute what was happening, she shoved her way past him and fell across the two children. A herd of other fans surged toward them, shouting, reaching, pushing. Feet scraped against concrete. Bodies slammed into seats.

Reaction set in. With split-second timing, Gabe blocked Brooke and the children with his body and shot one hand into the air to deflect the oncoming foul ball. The hard smack of leather against skin stung, but he held on.

A collective sigh of defeat went up from the surging crowd.

Some good sport slapped him on the back. "Good catch, man."

Shocked and amazed, Gabe opened his hand to a white ball against a stinging red palm.

The crowd ebbed away.

Gabe looked down at the pile of Brooke, Macy and A.J. Brooke was spread over the children like an unfurled umbrella. Below her, A.J.'s eyes were wide with shock. Macy's glasses were askew. Something sweet and bright flared in Gabe's chest. He took Brooke's arm and helped her up.

"That was close." She straightened Macy's glasses.

"Closer than you know." He held out the foul ball.

"Gabe! That ball was a rocket. How did you do that?"

"Reflex."

"That wasn't reflex," she insisted. "That was skill. Reflex was what I did."

He disagreed on that count. What she'd done came from the heart.

"Let me see your hand. It has to be red."

"It's nothing." He loved when she fussed over him.

"Look." Macy pointed at the big screen in center field. "There we are. We're on the big screen." She jumped up and down in excitement as Gabe's catch replayed and the stadium roared.

Brooke still held his hand. He could get used to this. "We'll get some ice at the concession."

"Brooke, don't take my man card. I can bare-hand a baseball."

She hiked an eyebrow, tickled. "Your man card?"

"Daddy got a boo-boo. Kiss it."

Both adults turned toward A.J. Macy giggled. "Yeah, kiss it, Brooke. Make it all better."

The thought of kissing put Gabe's brain on spin cycle. His gaze instantly went to Brooke's lips, lips he knew to be soft as velvet and sweeter than a fried Twinkie. Their gazes collided and held as Brooke's perfect lips curved knowingly.

"Later," she murmured, and then with a wink, she grabbed his hand and kissed the palm.

While his skin tingled from the touch of her lips, the single, intoxicating word tingled in his head. Later? What did she mean by later?

"Daddy, I go potty." The toddler's request drew his attention away from Brooke and the unnerving need to spend some alone time with the nanny.

He hoisted A.J. into one arm. "Potty first and then concession." He pointed at Brooke. "No ice."

She laughed and rolled her eyes. "Man card."

Gabe chuckled and started up the steps.

Surrounded by the mixed smells and sounds of an outdoor sporting event, they entered the prom-enade, a long balcony-like strip of concession area. The sun slipped over the mountains behind left field in a showy display. Stadium lights took over.

They stopped first at the restrooms, and then, like magnets, Macy and A.J. were pulled toward the souvenir stands. Gabe didn't mind. He wanted Macy to have good memories of tonight and a souvenir would help. So what if he bought Brooke a T-shirt to match his? She'd bought him a foam finger. With hands full of Rockies memorabilia, they joined the line to order eats and drinks.

While they waited, A.J. rocked back and forth, spun on one foot and jabbered to his new stuffed Dinger the Dinosaur about gummy snacks.

Macy fiddled happily with her team spirit bracelet, shaking the purple beads back and forth on her wrist, hugged her teddy bear and preened in her Rockies ball cap that matched Brooke's.

Times like this made all the years of hard work worth the effort. As a boy, he'd never been able to afford a baseball, much less a baseball game with souvenirs. He was glad he could give these things to the people he cared about.

He laced his fingers with Brooke's and enjoyed the moment. Content. Happy. Full of gratitude to God for finally bringing him out of the darkness the past four years had produced.

His cell phone jingled. He groaned. Please, no problems tonight when he was enjoying a great time with Brooke, the best time he'd had in years.

The voice on the other end was a familiar one.

"Reverend West?" he asked, curiosity rising. Why would the pastor be calling this late?

Brooke heard the name and lifted an eyebrow in question. Gabe shot a concerned look toward Macy and shook his head. Brooke frowned, sensing his unease. Fortunately, the little girl was distracted by the dozens of things going on around her and the pile of toys in her arms.

Heart sinking, Gabe listened to the message. "Okay. Where? When? As soon as we can."

He slid the phone closed and sighed. Why now, Lord? Why at all?

Brooke moved close and softly murmured, "Gabe?"

He took her arm and turned them slightly away from the children.

"It's Macy's mother."

"Darlene?"

He nodded, grimly. "She's been taken to the hospital."

Chapter Thirteen

The waiting room in the county hospital boasted six plastic chairs and a brown vinyl chair with a matching couch. A.J. lay sprawled asleep on the one stuffed chair while Macy sat in wide-eyed fear between Gabe and Brooke on the couch.

The trip from Denver had been made with Brooke and Gabe doing their best to reassure the frightened little girl, but the car had been thick with her worry. Now, they waited along with Reverend West and his wife for word that the testing was completed. According to the pastor, Darlene had left work early with a fever. When Mrs. West had gone to check on her, she'd found Darlene too ill to answer the door.

Systemic lupus was a disease Brooke knew little about. Apparently, Darlene's was serious, and now she was having something called a flare. Whatever it was, Macy's mother was quite ill.

"The Rockies won," Brooke said, half-heartedly pointing to the score. A television hanging from one wall displayed scenes from the baseball game. "Six to three."

The others gave the TV a listless glance. No one had the heart for baseball anymore.

They'd had such fun at the game and she'd entertained the notion that she and Gabe and A.J. could be a family. She'd dreamed of more outings with him, more time holding his strong, capable hand, more opportunities to explore the feelings growing between them.

Now, her desires seemed selfish, given what Darlene and Macy were going through.

Macy listlessly plucked at the fur on her teddy bear. "When can I see my mama?"

Brooke squeezed the child's knee. "Soon, sweetheart. As soon as the doctors have her all fixed up."

Lord, please hurry. This child is suffering.

The prayer was barely a thought when a nurse clad in blue scrubs came toward them. "Are you the family of Darlene Perry?"

"Friends, and this is her pastor," Gabe said.

Macy leaped to her feet. "She's my mommy."

"You must be Macy," the nurse said with a gentle smile. "Your mom is worried about you, so when you go in to see her can you do her a favor?"

Eyes wide behind her glasses, Macy nodded.

"We had to connect some tubes to her arms and nose. Don't be scared about that. They're helping her get better. Okay?"

Macy's throat bobbed. "Okay," she whispered.

Gabe stood, a hand on Macy's shoulder. "Can we see her now?"

"Room 114. Don't stay too long." To Reverend West, she said, "The doctor would like to speak with you, sir, if you don't mind waiting."

"Certainly." The pastor and his wife sat down again.

"Leave the baby asleep, Gabe," Mrs. West said. "I'll watch him."

Brooke and Gabe each took one of Macy's cold hands and went to Darlene's room. The air inside the cubicle swam with scents of alcohol swabs and medication. Darlene was as pale as the white sheets. A yellow fluid dripped with a steady ticktick into one arm.

Darlene opened her eyes and immediately reached a hand toward Macy. The little girl rushed to the bed and buried her face against her mother.

Brooke's heart hurt to watch. She remembered having a sick mother. She remembered wishing she could make things better.

She gripped Gabe's hand, felt his reassuring squeeze and was painfully glad for his company.

"Brooke."

Brooke moved close to the weak voice, taking Gabe with her.

"What can we do for you, Darlene?"

Tired eyes lifted to study Brooke's face as if gauging her sincerity. "Take care of my baby."

The request jolted Brooke. "You'll be up and around soon, Darlene. But sure, Gabe and I enjoy hanging out with Macy. We'll be glad to spend more time with her if that helps you." She snuck a peak at Gabe's grave face, hoping he agreed.

"No, you don't understand." Darlene moistened puffy lips. "Macy, baby, go wait with Reverend West. Let me talk to Brooke for minute."

"Can I come back?"

Darlene mustered a smile. "You better. I need a good night kiss."

Macy nodded and backed out of the room, probably not fooled by her mother's bravado.

As soon as the door closed, Darlene's focus returned to Brooke and Gabe, asking for something Brooke couldn't understand. "No one knows exactly what may happen with this disease. Or when. But the flares are getting worse."

"What does your doctor say?"

"That I could have a few weeks or a few years." She moved restlessly, rustling the sheets. "It's the few weeks that scare me. I'm not afraid to die. I'm afraid for Macy to be alone."

Gabe reached for the pale, puffy hand lying against the sheet. "She must suspect things aren't good."

"I want to prepare her but I don't know how. Will you—?" She pulled her hand from beneath Gabe's to grasp Brooke's arm in a frantic grip. "She admires you both so much. Talk to her, Brooke. Help her through this. She'll need you."

Brooke wanted to back away and say, "Me? Why me?" But she couldn't. The woman was in dire straits with few options, and for whatever reason, she'd fixated on Brooke helping Macy through a hard time.

Pulse thudding, she covered Darlene's fingers with hers. "If you'd like, she can stay with me until you're out of the hospital. Or anytime at all. Just say the word."

"Yes. Thank you. Thank you." The tension left Darlene. And as if she'd used every bit of energy she had left, her head dropped back against the pillows. She closed her eyes and said no more.

Gabe felt the trembling in Brooke's hand long after Darlene fell asleep and they'd tiptoed from the room. She must be as confused as he was. Darlene seemed intent on drawing him and Brooke into Macy's life. *Why them?*

"She has no one," Brooke said quietly as if she was thinking the same thing.

"Makes you realize how blessed you are, doesn't it?"

"Yes. I have family everywhere, most of which I haven't appreciated as much as I should."

"I hear ya." His family was small and he spent as much time as possible with them. Tonight, his efforts didn't seem enough. Family mattered.

"My heart breaks for Darlene. She's a mother who loves her child and knows she may not be around to care for her. And she's all the child has. The uncertainty must be horrible."

They entered the waiting area to find A.J. awake and fussy. He reached immediately for Brooke.

"A dad could get a complex," Gabe grumbled, but secretly he was thrilled with the way A.J. and Brooke had bonded. He'd done some bonding with his neighbor, too.

Brooke clasped A.J. to her shoulder and rocked while they spoke quietly with the Wests.

"We'll stay here as long as she needs us," the pastor offered. "Why don't you take the children home and let them get some rest?"

The idea had merit. After the long, exciting day, they were all dragging. "We'll bring Macy back tomorrow."

Reverend West clapped Gabe on the shoulder. "You're a blessing. Thank you for all you've done."

Under the circumstances, Gabe thought, it wasn't enough.

Late the next morning, with A.J. at his side carrying a sack of boxed juices, Gabe knocked twice at Brooke's back door and then slid the glass doors apart and entered the homey den. She knew he was coming. He'd phoned her the moment his eyes opened this morning after a surprisingly restful night. He'd expected to toss and turn and worry. Instead, he and Brooke and Macy had prayed together and he'd gone home and slept like a rock, with the added bonus of a very pleasant dream starring Brooke Clayton in a wedding dress. Funny how a dream could start a man thinking irrational, impossible thoughts.

"Country breakfast delivery," he called. "Compliments of the Hicks brothers, finest chefs in Clayton." Granted, Gerald and Jerome were the only chefs in Clayton, but anyone with taste buds would appreciate their breakfast fare. "Hash browns and biscuits. Bacon and eggs. Jelly and butter. And a giant side of cream gravy."

When neither Macy nor Brooke responded, he and A.J. went into the kitchen. Voices came from the adjacent living room. He deposited the white carryout boxes on the kitchen table and went on through to find the ladies.

His first clue that all was not well came from Macy. She was crying, hands over her face. She and Brooke sat on the floor. A hairbrush and a bunch of girly hair gadgets lay on the rug next to them. Brooke ran a soothing hand over the child's long, blond hair. Sitting close together that way, Gabe was struck by how perfectly their shades of blond matched.

"Tender-headed?" Gabe asked hopefully.

Brooke shook her head at him. "Meltdown."

He was afraid she'd say that. He'd dealt with plenty of meltdowns from Tara. He preferred to avoid these outbursts at all costs. But at least Macy had valid reasons for falling apart—unlike his late wife's fits of temper, which were brought on when she didn't get her way.

Gingerly, he lowered himself to the floor next to the little girl. "Hey, Miss Macy. How can I help?"

"My mama's going to die," she blurted and then burst into a fresh round of aching sobs.

Sweet A.J. patted her head. "Don't cwy, Macy. I give you juice."

Gabe swept his son onto his lap. "I can take him outside if we're in the way."

"Stay," Brooke said simply. "We need you."

We?

With a face wreathed in compassion, Brooke

said, "Macy, I know how you hurt. I know how scared you are."

"But I said that really mean stuff to her and after that she got sick again. I didn't mean it. I was just mad because she can't ever play."

"What did you say, Mace?" Gabe asked gently.

Macy covered her face again and sniffed. "If she dies it'll be my fault. She thinks I don't love her anymore, but I do."

"Macy, listen to me and listen good." Expression darkening, Brooke took Macy's arm and forced her to look up. "Your mother's illness has nothing to do with you. Nothing."

"She knows you love her," Gabe added.

"That's right and she would be heartbroken to think you blamed yourself for this flare in her lupus."

"But I said I needed a new mama who could take me places like you do. And she started crying. Then she got sick again." The child's guilt and misery were palpable. She removed her glasses and scrubbed at cheeks puffy with crying.

Brooke sat very still for several seconds studying the broken child. Then in a quiet, determined voice, she said, "Can I tell you a secret? One that I almost never share with anyone?"

Macy interest was piqued. So was his.

"When I was eight, my baby sister died. She was

two and a half, the most precious little girl." Tears gathered on Brooke's eyelids.

An unexplainable foreboding stirred inside Gabe. Two and a half. A.J.'s age. He battled the strong compunction to grab his son and both of his girls and run far and fast to spare them pain. His girls. One child, one woman. Both beautiful blue-eyed blondes who were hurting.

"What happened?" Macy asked, sniffing. "Something bad?"

"Something very bad." Brooke laced her fingers together, the pinky finally healed and unwrapped, though now the skin was white with pressure. "You know that creek behind my house? The one I won't ever take you to?"

Macy nodded.

Dread grew in Gabe's belly, heavy and dark. He didn't want to hear this story.

"Her name was Lucy. She was pretty like you, with lots of curls and a big, sweet smile. We all loved her but sometimes I got mad because people loved her best. Before she was born, I was the baby. I got the attention. Sometimes I wished she wasn't there."

"Brooke," he said, aching from the regret in her voice. "All kids are jealous of their siblings sometimes."

"And all kids say things and think things they don't mean." She drew in a deep breath and gazed into the distance as though seeing events play out inside her head. "My mother asked me to play with Lucy while she did laundry. I was supposed to be watching her. I was mad because I wanted to watch cartoons. She wandered down to the creek and fell in."

"Did she drown?" Macy whispered.

Brooke pressed her lips tightly together as fat tears shimmered on her eyelids. When she spoke the words were pained. "Yes. She drowned."

Gabe's heart fell to the bottom of his shoes and stayed there. The thought of losing A.J. was more than he could bear. The thought of what eight-year-old Brooke had seen and suffered was every bit as painful. Nothing he could do or say could erase the memory or the heartache.

He hated when he couldn't fix things.

He hugged A.J. closer, thankful for the warm, living child that he could just as easily have lost and almost had. As though he knew the seriousness of the conversation, A.J. leaned into his father and sat very still.

"You must have been really sad," Macy said.

"Sad. Scared. Guilty. Terribly guilty. I thought her death was my fault. I thought maybe I'd caused her death with my jealousy." Her fingers fiddled with a hair barrette, opening and closing and opening again. "I let that one memory hurt me for a long time. I don't want that to happen to you."

"When did you start feeling better?"

Brooke lay the barrette aside and pulled Macy into a hug. Over the child's head, her gaze locked with his. "Today."

Gabe's stomach lurched. She'd carried the guilt of her sister's death all these years. No wonder she'd resisted caring for A.J. It wasn't that she didn't like kids. Fear and guilt stood in the way.

"See, sweetie," Brooke went on. "I know how you feel, but I don't want you to carry this worry as long as I have. I want you to understand that you did nothing wrong. You did not cause your mother's illness. No matter what you said to her, she'll forgive you and love you forever. And you have to forgive yourself. Got it?"

"I'll tell her I'm sorry today."

"Great idea." Brooke stroked a long length of Macy's hair, letting her fingers linger on the ends. "We'll take her some pretty flowers, too, as an apology gift. How does that sound?"

"Okay, but—" She paused, fiddled with a pink hair band and then blurted, "Do you think my mama is going to die?"

Brooke lifted the child's chin. "We'll pray she won't. We'll pray every day."

"But what if she does?"

"Hey." Gabe could contain his compassion no longer. Arms around both, he drew them to his sides. They sat on the rug in a bundle of arms and snuggles, a foursome drawing comfort from one another. "She knows Jesus. She'll be okay, no matter what."

The answer didn't seem to be enough, but it was all he had.

After a long, throbbing time while the breakfast chilled and three hearts ached, Macy whispered the question swirling in Gabe's head. "If my mama dies, what's going to happen to me?"

"You're pretty amazing, you know that?"

Brooke held up a bottle of squirt mustard. "Because I make a mean sandwich?"

Gabe's mouth quirked. "Well, there is that, but no. What you did for Macy."

She was glad he was here, glad he'd taken the day off from his busy schedule to be here for Macy. For her, too. She needed him. His strong shoulder, his quiet confidence, his absolute faith were exactly what she needed today.

Telling Macy about Lucy, especially in front of Gabe, had not been easy. To her relief, there had been no censure in Gabe, only compassion and caring.

Emotionally drained, Brooke had stayed at the house while Gabe and Macy shopped for Darlene's flowers. While they were gone she'd prayed, she'd looked at Lucy's photos and she'd finally let go. Thank God she'd recognized the parallel between her own tenacious guilt and Macy's. Setting Macy free had freed her, too.

Now the little girl and A.J. played in the backyard while Brooke and Gabe fixed sandwiches for a picnic after the hospital visit. Considering the stress of last night and this morning, they needed a diversion.

She slapped two pieces of bread together and slid the sandwich in a baggie. "You helped. I'm glad you were here."

"Why didn't I know about Lucy's death?" he asked quietly.

"I thought I told you she died."

"If you did, you left out the major details." He put aside the pack of cheese and reached for the lettuce.

"Shame, guilt, grief. Those are hard to talk about." She stuffed the finished sandwich into a picnic basket. "All these years I felt responsible, and then this morning I looked at Macy, saw myself and knew how wrong that was." She tapped her chest and fought back tears. "For the first time since I was eight, I feel free."

Gabe pushed away from the counter to kiss her forehead. "You helped her. She helped you. God sure knows how to work things out, doesn't He?"

"When we let Him."

"I figured out something this morning, too." He looped an arm over her shoulder and let her lean.

She liked leaning into Gabe, relying on his strength. He was a man a woman could depend on. "What?"

"I thought you didn't like kids, but you never said that. You said you weren't good with them. Guess what? That's a lie. You're amazing."

"I've been afraid. Afraid something else would happen. Afraid of the pain of loving and losing. Isn't that stupid? To withdraw from a chance to love someone because of fear?"

Gabe was so quiet for a few seconds that Brooke could hear the soft thud of his heart and the hum of the refrigerator. Outside Macy said something and A.J. babbled in response.

"Gabe?"

"Thinking."

"About?" She levered back a little to see his face.

"What you just said about fear holding us back from love." He stroked a hand over her shoulder and down her arm. "I've never told you about A.J.'s mother."

Other than the woman's tragic death in a car accident, she knew nothing about Gabe's wife. "I've wondered."

Gabe stepped away, went to the patio doors, hands in his pockets, and gazed out at the playing children. He was so handsome, her heart raced from looking at him. This morning had been the strangest mix of joy and pain, but being with Gabe had made the pain easier to bear.

"My marriage isn't a great topic for dinner conversation." His shoulders rose and fell. "I fell in love with Tara when she was nineteen. I was twenty-six. She was flighty and bubbleheaded and charming as sin. She was also high maintenance and selfish, but I didn't see those qualities until after we married. That's when I realized she wanted a sugar daddy, a man to hand her credit cards and let her do whatever she wanted." He huffed derisively. "Talk about emasculating."

Brooke quietly pushed the sandwiches aside, wiped her hands and went to stand beside him. "I'm sorry. You're better than that."

"Guess not. Within a year I knew I'd made a mistake, but I don't believe in divorce. I'd married her. She was my wife. I had to make the best of it." He sighed deeply. "When she decided to have a baby, fool that I was, I thought a child would mature her and put our marriage back on track. When she got pregnant with A.J., I was the happiest man in Denver."

"A.J. has that effect on people."

"Everyone but his mother," he said bitterly.

"Oh, Gabe."

"He was a toy to dress up and shop for, and when she tired of playing, she ignored him. She never got up in the night with him. She refused to deal with the icky side of parenting, as she called it. A couple of times she went shopping and left him home alone."

"That's hideous. You must have been terrified."

"After the second time, I hired a live-in nanny, but I couldn't bring myself to ban Tara from him. She was his mother. I kept hoping and praying things would change. I begged her to attend counseling." He released a long, shuddering breath. "She laughed and said there was nothing wrong with her. I was the problem. She accused me of being an old stick in the mud who didn't know how to have fun."

He sounded sad and so alone. Brooke slid both arms around his trim waist and learned against his solid, sturdy back. The soft cotton of his shirt felt cool and smooth against her cheek. "I'm sorry."

"Me, too. It was a fiasco. A misery I couldn't fix. All I could do was pray for things to change. The day she died, she had A.J. with her. She'd told the nanny they had a playdate." He scoffed. "A.J. was about eight months old. Tara was the one doing the playing. A.J. was her smoke screen."

Brooke's stomach clutched. "She was seeing someone else?"

He nodded. "Police investigating the accident found text messages on her phone. She was texting her lover when the accident occurred. He wasn't her first, but idiot Gabe was the last to know."

"A.J. was with her? Was he okay?"

"Not at first." He put his hand over hers where they clasped together around his middle. "He was unconscious. Cuts and bruises everywhere. I was scared out of my mind."

"I know."

"Yes, you do." He slowly pivoted, bringing them heart to heart. "I thought I was going to lose him. He looked tiny and helpless connected to machines, his eyes swollen shut. I sat beside his bed, praying, crying, helpless."

Gabe hated being helpless. He was a doer and a fixer, a protector. To see his marriage crumble and his son severely injured must have tested his faith greatly. "Thank God he survived," Brooke said quietly.

"I thank Him every single day. Every day when that little guy wakes up with that big smile on his face without brain damage, without paralysis. I'm blessed and grateful." He turned them both toward the glass and toward the two playing children. "Look at him out there. I don't know what I'd do if anything happened to him."

The old familiar fear pushed into Brooke's thoughts, but she fought it down. *Nothing* was going to happen to A.J. Not on her watch.

Chapter Fourteen

The trip to the hospital proved less traumatic than the previous night. Darlene seemed to be responding to the antibiotics and steroids enough to reassure her daughter. By the time the foursome returned to Clayton, Macy's shy smile was back in place and she was eager for lunch in the town square.

Yellow daisies and bluebells lit a path as Brooke carried the picnic basket across the green expanse of grass to the gazebo. With childish shrieks of summer joy, Macy and A.J. rushed off toward the swings. Beside Brooke, Gabe toted an ice chest of drinks.

"Stopping for burgers would have been easier," he said, clumping the cooler onto the wooden table.

Brooke made a face. "But not nearly as much fun."

"Guys go for easy."

She laughed. "That is so not true. Nobody works as hard as you do. Easy is not the way you do anything."

"Tell that to my employees at the Lucky Lady. If not for the telephone, they'd probably fire me."

Brooke unpacked the sandwiches and lined them on the table. "They can't fire you. You're the owner."

"See how smart you are. No wonder I like you."

"Seriously, Gabe, thank you."

He lifted a brow. "For?"

"Today. Yesterday." *Every single moment that you've given me.* "I'm not sure I could have handled all this drama without you."

"You could have. You're stronger than you think, Brooke." He popped the top on a soda can, handed the drink to her and then opened another for himself.

"You sound like Arabella."

"Smart woman that cousin of yours." He toasted the air with the can.

"She's helped me a lot since I've moved back. I wish I could do the same for her." She'd told him about Jasmine's engagement.

"I'm an outsider so maybe I see things differently than you do, but this whole family feud business is out of hand. Why can't you bury the hatchet and move on?"

"Because Cade's side of the family won't let

us." He didn't understand, couldn't know the history of bad blood. "They've pulled devious tricks, told lies, done everything they could to make our side of the family miserable for years. Long before my generation was born. Now with the inheritance..."

"The trouble has to end somewhere. Why not with this modern-day Romeo and Juliet?"

"Don't romanticize this thing, Gabe," she said, a little more sharply than she'd intended. "A wedding between Cade and Jasmine will be disastrous. No one wants it but them. Marriage won't heal things. It will make them worse. Cade's family will treat her like trash because she's Arabella's foster daughter. She'll be miserable."

Gabe raised his hands in surrender. "Okay, I give up. We're here to have a good time. Let's not talk about your cousins anymore."

Brooke's head of steam fizzled. "I'm sorry. I shouldn't have snapped at you that way, especially when you're trying to be sensible about something that makes no sense at all. Forgive me?"

Gabe tilted his head, dark eyes twinkling. "I don't know. I'm pretty badly wounded. You may have to kiss me and make me feel all better."

"Blackmail." Brooke moved closer. "I think I like it."

"Me, too." His face lowered to hers for a brief, sweet kiss that left them both smiling. She could get used to this, to kissing Gabe Wesson, to spending every day with him.

"Now that's the way to end an argument."

"We weren't arguing." Reluctant to move away, Brooke tapped his chest with one finger. "We were discussing."

"I have discussions at work and I've never ended one of them with a kiss."

Brooke burst into laughter. "Now that's an image I don't want to think about."

"Me, either. We've had two tranquil days at the mine. No use messing it up by kissing the wrong person. You, however—" He leaned in for one more soft, sweet meld of lips.

Brooke closed her eyes and breathed him in, aware of sensation flowing through her. The rich scents of summer. The cold, sweet taste of cola. The warmth of a kiss and the strength of Gabe's hands holding her close. She felt cared for. Protected. Loved?

When the kiss ended and she opened her eyes, the colors seemed sharper, brighter, crisper.

That's what falling in love with Gabe had done for her. Her world had come into focus. Beauty was everywhere, even here in the hometown she'd once abandoned.

"Penny for your thoughts," he said, smiling softly into her eyes.

She shook her head. No use ruining a perfect

day with an unwanted declaration of love. "Just good thoughts. I love being here with you and the kids."

"Yes, same here." His smile turned serious and he studied her for several long seconds, long enough for Brooke to begin to wonder.

A child's shrill laugh drew their attention and the moment was lost.

Still, Brooke wondered. She was sure that Gabe had feelings for her. But was love too much to hope for?

A slight breeze ruffled the aspens next to the gazebo and fluttered the paper napkins. Gabe plunked a banana on each one.

"About time to call the troops," he said. "This old man is getting hungry."

Brooke watched the two children racing around the park. "They play together really well."

"Better than siblings."

"Way better than I played with mine, that's for sure." Satisfied the table was set and the food ready, Brooke parked on the hard, concrete picnic bench. "Darlene seemed to have rallied today, but I can't stop wondering what will happen. Macy has no one."

"No use speculating." Gabe joined her, took one of her hands and kneaded her fingers. That simple contact was like a lifeline flowing between them.

Could he feel it, too? "The doctor says she could have years."

"Or months. Her kidneys aren't in good shape. Darlene seems to think she's fading. You can hear the worry in her voice, see it in her eyes. She's scared for her child."

"There's a real chance Macy's going to need a family, Brooke, to be there for her if the worst happens."

Macy could very well become an orphan. "Darlene seems intent on *us* looking after Macy as if we're relatives of some sort. She should be searching for an adoptive family, not two unrelated strangers." She sighed. "Darlene knows other people in Clayton better than she knows you or me. Why us? Why does she seem determined for us to take of care her daughter?"

"There's no accounting for matters of the heart, Brooke, and the care of her child is certainly a matter of the heart."

"True." Still, the whole issue seemed strangely unsettling.

"You could take her," he said, attention riveted on the palm of her hand. He traced a line with one finger.

Brooke's heart bumped. She pulled her hand away. "Me? You mean the way Arabella took in Jasmine?"

"No, not exactly." He took his time as if searching for exactly the right words. "I mean adopt her and give her a family."

"But she needs a mother *and* a father."

"That's what I was thinking." On the concrete picnic bench, he shifted closer, tilted her chin, probed her gaze with his. "A.J. needs a mother and a father, too."

Brooke's pulse kicked into overdrive. What was going on here? "He has a great dad."

"He needs a mom. A warm, funny, energetic mother who loves him the way he loves her."

Convinced her heart was about to fly from her chest, Brooke was afraid to say anything. Did he mean what she thought he meant? And if he did, if he was asking her to be A.J.'s mother, what about love? What about the two of them? She wanted to be more to Gabe Wesson than a mother to his son. She wanted to be his forever.

She opened her mouth to tell him exactly that when his cell phone chirped.

Gabe groaned in exasperation. "Some days I want to throw this thing in the river." With a sigh, he answered. "Wesson. This better be good."

Brooke's giggle froze in her throat when Gabe slapped the telephone closed. "Gotta go. Sorry about the picnic."

"What's wrong?"

"Not sure. Trouble in the mine shaft. If you'll

give me your car keys, I'll have someone bring your car around."

"We can bum a ride or walk. Home is not that far."

He stuck out his palm. "Give me the keys."

She dug in her jeans and handed over the cross key ring. "Thoughtful of you. Thanks."

He gave her a funny look. "A man takes care of his own."

Brooke opened her mouth, closed it again. Now was not the time, but the time was coming. She shoved a sandwich in his hand. "Call me? Let me know what's going on?"

He paused, smiled down at the sandwich, then leaned in and kissed her. "Absolutely."

Then he was gone and she was left to ponder that one tantalizing phrase.

A man takes care of his own.

The picnic wasn't nearly as much fun after Gabe's departure, but Brooke saw to it that her charges ate a hearty lunch and had a good time. After her car arrived and the kids had played out, she took them to the post office and the grocery store to stock up on the boxed juices and fruits Macy and A.J. favored. And if she tossed in a package of Oreos, she blamed Gabe for her fall from health-food glory. The man could eat his weight in cookies and never gain an ounce.

Inside the small, family-owned grocery, Brooke paused over and over again to visit with people she'd known since childhood. One woman exclaimed about how much she looked like her father, a declaration Brooke found discomfiting. George Clayton Jr. was an image in her mind, a distant figure she'd yearned for, but he'd never been a father like Gabe.

At the checkout counter, Macy helped unload the cart while Brooke chatted with the cashier. The friendly woman had given both kids a smiley sticker and allowed Macy to come behind the counter to help bag the items. The simple, friendly kindness made Macy feel important and reminded Brooke of the good things a small town offered that she'd never encountered in a city.

By the time they left the grocery store, A.J. rubbed at his eyes, ready for a nap.

"Soon, little man," she said, strapping him into his car seat.

As she loaded groceries into the car, a voice called her name. "Brooke, hello. I was just about to call you."

The pastor's wife came toward her, pumps tapping as she hurried her pace. Dressed in a classic beige pantsuit with her short dark hair neatly coiffed around a serene face, Laura West was the poster child of ministers' wives—warm, gracious and genteel.

A frisson of alarm rushed up Brooke's arms. "Mrs. West, is everything all right?"

Macy popped out of the backseat, eyes wide. "Is my mama—?"

"Your mama is doing great," Mrs. West reassured. Then to Brooke she said, "Reverend West asked me to track you down if I could. He told me about your phone call and agrees one hundred percent. He can visit with Macy this afternoon."

Brooke's anxiety drained away. Confident Reverend West would handle the situation better than she could, Brooke had requested counseling for Macy. Given the trauma she was enduring from Darlene's illness and the terrible uncertainty, the child needed all the wisdom they could provide.

"That's terrific."

"But first—" Mrs. West tapped Macy's nose with one finger "—you and I are going shopping for those shoes you need. Something about a pair of sneakers with hot pink laces?"

"How did you know?" Macy asked and then immediately said, "Mama told you."

"Yes, she did."

"I can take her, Mrs. West."

"Of course you could, Brooke, but I can't let you have all the fun with Macy, can I?"

The pastor's wife warmed Brooke's heart. There were some fine people in this town. Funny how she'd forgotten that. "A.J. is long overdue for a nap, so I suppose this is great timing."

"The Lord knows what we have need of," the woman said. "Ready, Macy?"

Macy's face glowed from the special attention as she and Mrs. West headed down the street.

When Brooke arrived home and began unloading groceries and picnic items, she settled A.J. on a pile of pillows in front of his Mozart video hoping he'd fall asleep on his own. He seemed to love the soothing music and gentle visuals of puppets and toys.

When Brooke bent to kiss his cheek, he hugged her neck. "I love you, A.J."

"Lub you, Mama."

Brooke froze, emotion washing through her, warm and wonderful and disconcerting. A.J. had no idea what he'd just done. He'd heard the word from Macy a dozen times today. Nonetheless, Brooke pressed the word against her heart and let imagination take flight.

What if Gabe loved her? What if she could be his wife and A.J.'s mother? She'd gladly give up her share of the inheritance and anything else she owned to be loved by this special father and son.

Rosy with the good feelings, she left A.J. cuddling his fluffy yellow duck while she put away the groceries and unpacked the picnic basket.

When a knock sounded at the front door, she

shoved the milk in the refrigerator and cast a quick glance into the den. Satisfied that A.J. was content, she hurried through the house to answer the knock.

Humming, happy, thinking of Gabe's kiss and A.J.'s sweet love, she clicked the lock and pulled open the door.

No one was there.

A buzz of adrenaline, like an electric shock, stung her nerve endings. Cautiously, she looked through the glass and onto the porch. No one. All was quiet in the neighborhood.

The wind chime swayed. But the leaves on the trees were still.

A chill rushed down Brooke's spine. She stepped out on the porch to look around. "Hello? Anyone there?"

Going quickly to the end of the porch she looked down the side of the house. A new white spot, compliments of Gabe, was all that remained of the frightening episode of red spray paint and a hooded visitor no one had ever identified.

Goosebumps prickled her arms. She had the creepiest feeling someone was watching.

Unnerved by the thought, she hurried back inside and shut and locked the door. Mozart drifted through the rooms and into her consciousness. A terrible, sick foreboding came with it.

"A.J." She broke into a run. "A.J.!"

She skidded to a stop inside the den, heart pounding, mouth dry. Her world crumbled. The childhood nightmare started again.

A.J. was gone.

Chapter Fifteen

Gabe feared his head would explode. "Tell me again."

He'd driven like a maniac from the mine, praying he'd misunderstood Brooke's nearly incoherent voice quivering through the telephone line. Now, as he stood in Brooke's den, he still couldn't believe this was happening.

He grabbed Brooke by the arms. "From the start."

Eyes frantic and wide, she trembled like an aspen in a windstorm. "Someone knocked on the door. No one was there. When I came back A.J. was gone. The patio doors were open."

"Call the sheriff. Call everyone you know." Punching numbers into the phone he bolted outside and ran from Brooke's yard to his. "A.J.! A.J.!"

The terror inside him grew into a monster,

tearing at his insides, threatening to steal his sanity. He'd come close to losing A.J. once before. This couldn't be happening.

Vaguely he heard Brooke's voice calling, too. She was always diligent to the point of obsession with A.J. How could this have happened? How could she have allowed it to happen?

He raced around the house, calling, only to meet Brooke in the front yard.

"He's not there. He's not here." Near hysteria, Brooke clawed at his arm. "The door was shut, Gabe. How did he get outside?"

"That's what I want to know." Beginning to shake, he fought fear and lost. Where was his son? "How could this happen? Where *were* you?"

The stricken look on her face slapped at him, but he was too scared to apologize.

"I told you. He was safe in the den, exhausted from the park. I promise, Gabe, he was almost asleep. Someone knocked at the door. I went to answer."

"Who?"

Frustrated, crying now, she moaned. "No one was there. How could he get outside? The door was closed. He can't open it by himself, can he?"

"I don't know. He's doing more and more on his own. He can open the bathroom door. Maybe…" He pressed a fist against his lips. With a deep groan of misery, visions of A.J. after the car accident flashed through Gabe's head. Not again. *Please Lord, wherever he is, keep him safe.* "He can't be that far away."

Brooke gasped. Color drained from her cheeks. "Oh, no. Oh, no, no, no! The creek!"

She broke into a run. Gabe jammed his cell phone into a pocket and raced after her, heart thundering, mouth dry with terror. *Not the creek. Dear God, not the creek. He's only two.*

Silver Creek ran a dozen yards behind their homes. Generally a low-flowing stream, rains or melting snow from the mountains could swell the water to several feet.

A hard rain had fallen this week.

His boots thudded heavily against the overgrown weeds and grass. Brooke, with her athlete's form and tennis shoes outdistanced him. She reached the stream first and ran wildly along the bank. He heard her gulping sobs as he approached.

"Any sign?"

"Nothing." But she kept moving.

"A.J. Where are you? A.J.? Come to Daddy."

The trickle and babble of Silver Creek was his only answer.

Breathless from the run, Gabe stood with hands on hips, panting, adrenaline jacked to supersonic speed as he searched the rolling terrain between his home and the mountains beyond. A forest line bordered the mountains beyond the creek.

"He can't have gone to the woods," Brooke said, following his gaze. She was breathless, too, though more from crying than the run. "We'll find him, Gabe. I'm sorry. Terribly sorry. I know I've let you down. I love him. I would never let anything happen to him."

"But you did." The words were out before he could stop them. They were unfair and cruel and though he wished them back immediately, the damage was done. With a sharp cry of hurt, Brooke spun away to continue the search.

Miles of field and unimproved terrain surrounded this neighborhood on the edge of town. As far as his eye could see were grass and flowers and fences, but no small boy.

Leaving Brooke to search this vector, he jogged back to the house. The sheriff was on his way. He'd want information. And some small part of him kept hoping to find A.J. playing in his room or on the patio. None of this made sense. Not Brooke's explanation. Not the sudden, swift, complete disappearance of a toddler too small to get far on his own. Where *was* he?

Protect him, Lord. I feel so helpless.

By the time he entered his yard cars and people lined the drive, the adjacent street and half the lawn. For once he was glad bad news travels fast.

Gabe went immediately to the sheriff standing

beside the police car. The lawman would probably be relieved to retire and put these past few weeks of trouble behind him. As yet, there was no one to replace him, a worry for Gabe and all the citizens of Clayton. Today just proved how badly the town needed law enforcement.

"Anything?" Gabe asked, voice tight with checked emotion.

Diggers pocketed a radio. "Not yet, but half the town is out looking. We'll find him."

"Do you need a photo?"

The sheriff gave him a long look. "This here is Clayton, son. We know the boy. He's one of ours. Not a soul will rest in this town until he's found."

Something broke inside Gabe at the sheriff's words. He slid to the ground by the cruiser and put his face in his palms. A heavy hand clamped on his shoulder. The support was all he needed to pull himself together.

"Sorry."

"No need. Now, tell me everything you know."

Gabe repeated Brooke's story.

Sheriff Diggers frowned. "Someone knocked but no one was there. Hmm." The officer hitched his pants. "Funny goings on around here lately. Guess I better speak to Brooke." He nodded toward the forlorn figure coming across the field.

"Right." Gabe pushed to a stand, unwilling to

face Brooke just yet. "I'll head the other direction. Call me if you hear anything."

Sheriff Diggers held out a hand. "You stay put. If the boy wandered off he might come wandering back."

"A.J.'s not even three years old. He's too small to go far." He blew out a frustrated gust of air. "That's why this makes no sense. If what Brooke says is true, she wasn't away from him more than two or three minutes. How far can a toddler stray in such a small amount of time? She would have been able to find him immediately."

The sheriff removed his hat and scratched at his head. "Well, I wasn't going to bring up the possibility just yet, but you've had your share of troubles at the Lucky Lady. And someone painted up the side of Brooke's house after she'd been with you. Seems to me, someone wants that mine shut down pretty badly. Desperate people do desperate things."

The idea had been rolling around inside Gabe's head ever since Brooke's call, but he'd refused to let it form. Now, he couldn't hold the thought at bay.

"You think A.J.'s been—" The word "kidnapped" stuck in his throat.

"I'd say it's a possibility we can't ignore, given all we know. You're a wealthy man." Diggers replaced his hat, giving the brim a careful adjustment. "Figure you better stick close to the house, just in case."

In case a kidnapper called or sent a message. The unspoken statement burned through Gabe like a flaming arrow, sharp and hot. This was far worse than the car accident. At least then he'd known A.J. was getting the best care possible. Now, if someone had him, he could be scared, hurt...or worse.

Sweat broke out on Gabe's body. Chills prickled the hairs on his arms. He prayed, half-baked attempts to calm the unwanted images flicking through his mind.

Car doors slammed. More people arrived. He recognized some. People from church. Store owners. The vet, a Brit everyone called Tweed because of his ever-present tweed cap. A handful of cowboy types.

Gabe's foreman hopped out of a company truck and strode across the lawn, followed by other mine workers. "We shut down. Figured you needed us here."

Touched, grateful, he said, "Thanks, Tim. I do."

A man of few words and plenty of action, the burly redhead gripped Gabe in a quick hug. A lump formed in Gabe's throat. These were good people, fine men.

"What's the baby wearing?"

Gabe repeated the description he'd been giving everyone. "Red shirt, jean shorts, green Crocs."

"Best get started." Tim gave quick, short directions to the gathered crew. "I'll search Chickadee Drive. Jed, you head east. Shane, take the creek."

"We've searched the creek," Gabe said.

"Won't hurt to look again." As he did every day at the mine, Tim quietly organized the others and then jumped into his truck. "Me and the boys know this area like the back of our hands. We'll find him, Boss."

Gabe couldn't bring himself to repeat the sheriff's concern that A.J. wasn't lost. He was stolen. He had to believe his son had simply toddled after a butterfly or a stray pup and gotten lost. The thought that someone might do harm to his child nearly broke him.

Dust swirled as trucks and cars and four-wheelers exited the driveway, each searcher going different directions.

Gabe tried not to think about the myriad dangers of this rugged country, dangers that had nothing to do with disgruntled humans. Within a mile radius, besides the deadly creek that had already claimed a small life, woods and mountains, old mining vents, abandoned railroad cars and wild animals waited to steal his child.

Across the yard, Brooke sat on her front porch

step, head tilted to speak with the sheriff. She was crying again. Had she ever stopped? Pity and the need to protect rose up in Gabe's chest. He wanted to go to her so badly, to hold and comfort and kiss away the tears. But after the harsh things he'd said, he couldn't. His brain was too full. His emotions too raw. He needed everything he had not to lose control and shatter into a million pieces.

An hour passed. A long, agonizing hour while he paced the yard, the house, the neighborhood. He searched and then re-searched under beds and inside closets, behind the couch, in Brooke's car, in her garage. People swarmed in and out with nothing to report.

"Sorry, Gabe," they'd say, shamefaced as if they'd failed. *They* hadn't failed him, but someone had.

Brooke isn't to blame, his conscience said. She loves A.J. She'd give her life for his. You know she would.

He didn't know what to think, what to do. A.J.'s mother had nearly killed him with her negligence. Now this.

He closed his eyes. Too distraught for rational prayer, he could only chant, "Bring him home, Lord. Bring him home."

"Gabe." At the touch of a soft hand, he looked up. Brooke.

"Gabe!" someone else shouted.

Spinning away from Brooke's tragic expression, he spotted the sheriff coming toward him in a lope. Linden Diggers was smiling.

"Found him."

"Oh, thank God." Brooke slung her arms around Gabe. "They found him. They found him. Gabe, they found him."

His knees threatened to buckle. A mass of emotion, afraid he'd fall apart, he stood like a rock. "Where? Is he all right?"

"Sounds to be. Kylie Jones found him over at her fiancé's place. Little fella wandered up in the backyard."

Brooke spun toward the sheriff. "He walked a quarter of a mile to Vincent's house? I don't believe it."

Gabe didn't take time to think. He ran to his vehicle.

Heart sinking, Brooke watched Gabe drive away. She understood his fear. She'd felt it, too, but he'd gone cold as ice, distancing himself as though he couldn't bear to look at her. He blamed her; that much was clear. She blamed herself. She should never have left the child alone, even to answer the door.

Needing to see with her own eyes that A.J. was all right, she jumped in her car and roared down Bluebird Lane toward her cousin's home. When she arrived, Gabe was there, long strides eating up the ground as he hurried toward Vincent's porch. The sheriff cruised in right behind Brooke.

Kylie Jones came out of the house, carrying A.J. He was eating a red popsicle.

Brooke's heart leaped with joy. He looked okay. He was safe. She hadn't lost him forever, not like she'd lost Lucy.

"Thank you, Jesus," she whispered as Gabe grabbed his son and hugged him close.

She ran to them, threw her arms around the pair and breathed in the living warmth of the child she'd come to love as her own and the man who held her world in the palm of his hand.

Gabe stiffened. A little piece of Brooke's heart broke, but right now, the thrill of A.J.'s safe return overshadowed everything else.

"I love you, A.J. Brooke is sorry you got lost."

A.J. babbled something and Gabe pulled away, turning to Kylie. "What happened? How did he get all the way out here?"

"I'm not sure," Kylie said, green eyes wide and worried. "I was in the kitchen when I heard a noise outside. Vincent gets strays dumped out here sometimes so I went to check, and there he was, sitting right over there." She pointed toward a corner of the house. "Next to that bush. He wasn't crying or anything, but he sure seemed glad to see me. He's such a sweetie."

At that moment, Vincent exited the house. Kylie's gaze bounced to her fiancé. She pressed her lips tight, saying no more.

Vincent shot a cocky glance toward Brooke before sauntering confidently up to Gabe. "We found him for you, Boss. Called you the minute Kylie spotted him."

"I don't know how to thank you," Gabe said, offering a hand.

Distaste curled in Brooke's belly. Vincent was not a man to do good deeds, but he knew how to take credit. What stunned her was the way everyone fell for his charm, even Gabe.

"No problem, Boss. Little tike could get hurt wandering that far from home. Glad we could be the ones to save him, all things considered." He shot another pointed look toward Brooke. She didn't buy his con for a minute. He had to be involved somehow. She glared, telegraphing her disbelief.

The sheriff came striding up, hat dusting the side of his uniform pants. "What happened here?"

"Well." Vincent looped an arm over Kylie's shoulders. "The way me and my fiancée see it, Gabe's little boy must have strayed from home. We're mighty glad he made it safely here to responsible people like Kylie and me. No telling what might have happened if the wrong person had found him. Who was supposed to be watching him anyway?"

The snide remark, clearly aimed at her, threw Brooke into a rage. She flew at him, finger stabbing the air in front of his nose. "You did this. You knocked on my door to distract me and then you took him."

Vincent caught her finger and laughed in her face. Brooke yanked away from his painful grip.

"You must think I'm some kind of a superhero if I could knock on your door and steal a kid at the same time." With an arrogant shrug, he sent a wide, overly sincere gaze around the circle of adults as if to say, "See what I have to endure from this crazy woman?"

Furious and frustrated, Brooke's fisted her hands at her sides so he couldn't see them shake. "I don't care how much you lie, Vincent. I believe you're responsible." She spun toward the sheriff. "Ask him where he was an hour ago. He did this, sheriff. He took that baby."

Vincent guffawed. "Now why would I do that, Brookey?"

She whirled on him. "Shut up. You just shut up and stop lying."

Gabe caught her arm. "Settle down. You're not helping."

"He did this, Gabe."

"Now, Brooke," the sheriff warned. "We know

about the bad feelings between your families, but accusing a man of kidnapping is serious."

"Ask him."

"All right. Vincent, I believe you, boy. I know you didn't have anything to do with this child getting lost. You been here all afternoon?"

"Sure have. Isn't that right, honey?" Vincent squeezed Kylie closer, his muscles bulging across her slim shoulders.

All Kylie said was, "I'm glad we found him."

"There we go then," Sheriff Diggers said. "Case closed. The important thing is this child is safe and sound, back in the care of his father. Now, let's get over to Wesson's place and spread the word. Lots of good folks still out there searching."

Police gear rattling at his hip, he pivoted and headed toward his cruiser.

Without a word to Brooke, Gabe and A.J. followed.

Gabe didn't sleep much that night or the next two nights. Plagued with what-might-have-happened, he'd taken A.J. into his own bed and then lay awake watching him breathe. As thankful as he was that his son had been found alive and well, he couldn't get the circumstances out of his mind. Something didn't jibe.

He'd contemplated a monetary reward for Vincent and Kylie, and considering the upcoming wedding, he'd probably follow through, but he remembered the look on Kylie's face and the way she'd seemed hesitant to back Vincent's story. Was his employee lying about something? Or was he simply glad to put Brooke in a bad light?

With an exhausted sigh, he pushed the covers away and went to the window. The stars were out tonight in force, a glory of God's universe, numbered and named by the Creator. Gabe wanted to appreciate the Lord's handiwork more but he felt too heavy inside.

Dawn would come soon. Today, he had to find a way to get back to work. The mine project was at a standstill, but leaving A.J. was out of the question.

His thoughts went to Brooke. He'd started to cross the lawn a dozen times. He'd opened his phone to call, but each time he'd reconsidered. He'd hurt her, said ugly things and he couldn't forget her look of devastation when he'd driven away with A.J., leaving her alone with Vincent and Kylie and her guilt. He knew she felt responsible. She'd struggled with guilt over her sister's death for years.

And she'd just now let go.

She didn't need a guy like him to bring it all back.

He didn't blame her. Not really. He was afraid. Afraid to take another chance. Afraid of losing

A.J. Afraid that whatever evil swirled around the mine and Brooke would harm his son. He'd never been a coward, but two scares were too many.

"I miss her."

She was hurting. As if she were an extension of himself he could feel her heartache because it was his own. He wondered if she was awake.

Three days seemed like a million.

He shouldn't have walked away and left her there.

Slowly, the stars went out, tiny blinks that disappeared like snuffed candles as dawn crept over the mountains. Gabe dressed, made coffee and waited for A.J. to awaken. Maybe he should move back to Denver for a while to be near his mother. Someone else could manage the mine operation—if he didn't shut it down completely.

No, he couldn't do that. Shutting down would put people out of work. Men like Tim and Shane and Jed who'd been there when he needed them to search for A.J. No matter how wealthy, a man couldn't buy that kind of loyalty. This little town cared, and in turn, he cared.

Feet propped on a kitchen chair, he scrubbed a hand over blurry eyes. The back of his neck hurt. His heart hurt worse.

His cell phone chirped. At six o'clock in the morning, this couldn't be good news. He frowned at the unfamiliar number.

"Gabe Wesson."

"Wesson? Zach Clayton."

Gabe's feet thudded to the floor. "Brooke's brother?"

"Right."

An uncomfortable silence hummed across the miles. What could Brooke's law dog brother want with him at six o'clock in the morning?

Chapter Sixteen

Her bag was packed. The house locked. Her brother and sister informed of her whereabouts. A weekend in Colorado Springs might be what she needed to clear her head and make a firm decision. Since the disaster with A.J. and Gabe, she'd waffled back and forth about leaving town for good. The inheritance meant nothing without Gabe and A.J. At the same time, others depended on her. Macy for one. Arabella for another. As far as she could figure, none of the other heirs to Grandpa George's fortune were ever coming home anyway.

With a final, longing glance toward Gabe's quiet home, she put the Toyota in reverse and backed out of the driveway. She'd watched Gabe come and go for three days, watched him sit in broody silence on his back patio until she felt like a stalker.

The relationship growing between them had

died when she'd let him down in the worst possible manner.

Didn't he know she loved him? Didn't he know she would protect A.J. with her life?

But she hadn't. Whether by accident or design, A.J. had disappeared under her care. Nothing could change that. How could she expect forgiveness from Gabe when she couldn't forgive herself?

The car bumped across the train tracks as she turned onto Railroad Street. Jasmine had asked to meet at the café this morning before she left. Brooke didn't have the heart for breakfast or conversation, but Jasmine needed a friend, considering the wall of resistance she and Cade had slammed into when they'd announced their upcoming nuptials.

Jasmine was already there, seated at a table in the center of the room when Brooke stepped inside. Bacon scented the air. Brooke's stomach growled, a reminder of the meals she hadn't eaten.

"Are you okay?" Jasmine asked when Brooke scooted a chair up to the table. "You look really tired."

"Rough few days."

Erin, the café owner, stopped at the table, pencil and pad ready. "What are you having, Brooke?"

"Coffee."

Erin jacked an eyebrow. "That's all? No breakfast? No sweet rolls? We got fresh honey buns."

"Coffee's fine, thanks." She couldn't swallow food if her life depended on it.

"Jerome is not going to be happy," Erin mumbled but she retrieved the carafe and filled Brooke's cup. "How's Gabe's little boy doing?"

Brooke averted her gaze, embarrassed to admit she and Gabe were no longer communicating. "Fine."

"Good. Quite a scare." The proprietress moved on to top off other coffee cups and visit with her customers.

Jasmine squeezed her hand on the tabletop. "I'm so glad everything worked out. We were all frantic with worry. You must have been terrified. Cade and some of the other ranch hands had saddled horses, ready to search where cars couldn't when the call came in that A.J. been found."

"That was nice of him."

"He really is a wonderful man, Brooke."

"I believe you."

"I wish Arabella would." Jasmine fiddled with a napkin, taking an inordinate amount of time spreading the thin sheet of paper over her lap. "I have a favor to ask."

Brooke smiled a little. "The last time you said that, you caused an explosion."

"I want you to be my bridesmaid."

Brooke blinked. "Me?"

All the reasons she shouldn't agree rushed in. Being a bridesmaid was taking sides, giving in to the wedding no one in her family wanted. Arabella would be upset.

"Yes, you. You're the only one who's been able to say one nice thing about Cade and the way he treats me. You've been fair and open-minded." Brooke wasn't sure how much of that was true. "Besides, you know how it feels to be in love."

The reminder was a knife through the heart. She did know how Jasmine felt. The love she had for Gabe was a beautiful thing, whether he could accept it or not. Loving him and A.J., though she ached now, was worth everything.

"All right, Jasmine. You have yourself a bridesmaid."

Jasmine squealed and jumped up from the table to give Brooke a hug. The teen's joy chased some of Brooke's depression away.

"Well, look who we have here. If it isn't my irresponsible cousin, Brookey."

At the sound of Vincent's snide voice, Brooke's stomach clenched. Pretending not to hear, she hugged Jasmine again and sat down to her coffee. "Let's talk flowers and colors and all that fun stuff."

Vincent's bulky form appeared at her elbow. "You can run but you can't hide, cousin."

"Leave her alone, Vincent," Jasmine said.

"After what she accused me of? Not likely. Especially when she's the guilty party." His voice rose. Heads in the café turned. "Everybody in town wonders if Gabe Wesson is crazy for hiring you to nanny his son. What kind of man does that? Or maybe he didn't know how you let your own baby sister drown."

All the blood drained from Brooke's head. Dizzy, ears roaring, the need to rush out of the café and as far from Vincent as possible was powerful. She started to rise.

Jasmine grabbed her hand, held her in place. "Don't listen to him."

"She'd better listen. Everyone is talking about what a catastrophe she is." By now he was no longer speaking to Brooke but to the customers in the crowded café. "First, she lets her tiny baby sister die. Then she loses my boss's son and tries to lay the blame on me, the one who found him. Something is seriously wrong with a woman like that."

Humiliation burned hot inside Brooke. She pushed the chair back and stood, eager to escape.

"Go ahead, cousin, run away like you always do."

She'd been poised to do exactly that but Vincent's words had a strange effect. He wanted her to run. He wanted to make her afraid. With a strength she didn't know she possessed, she faced her childhood tormentor.

"I'm not going anywhere, Vincent. This time you can't scare me. I've made mistakes but they were honest ones. You, however, are a liar and a troublemaker. You had far more to do with A.J.'s disappearance than I did."

Vincent threw his muscled arms out to the side. "See? She blames me for her mistakes. She can't keep up with one little kid and it's all my fault."

"Admit it, Vincent, here and now in front of all these people. You want me to leave town so you can inherit my grandfather's fortune. That's what this is all about. You and Marsha and Billy Dean and Cousin Les have conspired and you're the ring leader just the way you've always been."

"You're paranoid. Crazy."

"All I want to know is why you had to drag Gabe into your web of evil? I pray to God I haven't been the one to bring trouble down on his head, but you're the one who took A.J. and you're the one causing problems at the mine. You and your hateful family. And I won't rest until I prove it."

Vincent laughed, a mocking, hateful sound. "What makes you think Gabe will believe an airhead who can't even keep up with her house keys? Give it up, Brooke, and crawl back to wherever you've been hiding."

"You go too far, Vincent. It's time for this bitterness to stop. It's time for you to stop."

"Oh?" He strutted like the peacock he was. "Who's going to stop me? You?"

"Me."

Brooke spun toward the beloved voice. With emotions running high, she hadn't even heard the bell jingle, but Gabe stood in the doorway.

And he was furious.

"I heard everything, Vincent." Gabe kept his tone low and controlled, though the protector in him wanted to throttle Brooke's cousin. He lowered A.J. to the floor and boosted him toward the woman who loved him. "Go to Brooke, A.J."

"Boss, hey." Vincent touched his chest, ingratiating. "Great to see you."

"I bet."

"I don't know what you thought you heard, but this bimbo who nearly got your boy killed has gone off the deep end this morning. She's crazy, accusing me when she's the guilty party."

Gabe snapped. He grabbed Vincent by the collar. "That *bimbo* happens to be the woman I love, the woman who tried to warn me against you, but I didn't listen. I'm listening now."

Vincent sputtered, his face mottled with rage. "She's trying to get me fired."

"You know what? It worked. You're fired."

Vincent slapped at Gabe's hands and knocked them away. Enraged he glared at Brooke. "This isn't over."

Then his former employee stomped out of the café.

The room pulsed silent, a sharp contrast to the roar in Gabe's head. He gazed around at a dozen faces staring wide-eyed at the scene played out in public. Gerald had come out of the kitchen, frying pan aloft.

Gabe shook his head. "Sorry folks. This is not the way I usually do business."

"Not your fault. Vincent needed taking down a notch." Gerald lowered the frying pan. "He had no business treating Brooke like that. Man shouldn't disrespect a woman."

"I couldn't agree more." Gabe's gaze found the one he'd been defending. The corners of her mouth softened, though she stayed where she was. Cheeks blanched white from the confrontation, she clasped A.J. to her shoulder. A.J. clung like a monkey.

The realization of how much he'd hurt her tore through Gabe. He'd put that haunted look in her beautiful blue eyes. Could she forgive him? Would she?

"Brooke." He held out a hand. "I'm sorry."

Her face crumbled.

Gabe took two steps, opened his arms and pulled

her and A.J. close. Her trembling body made him mad all over again. "You okay?"

She sighed. "I am now."

He kissed the top of her head. "Can we talk?"

Her voice was a whisper. "Maybe somewhere else?"

"I don't care who hears. I want the world to know how I feel."

She pulled back and looked into his face. "How do you feel?"

Every confused emotion melted away. He knew what he wanted, what he needed. "I was a first-rate jerk the other day. I owe you an apology."

Her head dropped. "I see."

"I don't think you do." He tilted her chin. "Maybe we *should* do this in private."

Jasmine, standing by with a shocked expression and a slight smile, shoved a purse into Brooke's free hand. "Go. No one's in the park."

As they made their exit, Gabe was certain he heard a collective sigh go up inside the café.

Brooke was a mess of emotions. She'd never stood up to Vincent before and the resulting shakes still buckled her knees. But she'd crawl across the street to be with Gabe and hear what he had to say. Hope springs eternal was a proverb for a reason.

They reached the empty gazebo and released

the wiggling boy, who'd spotted the playground as they crossed the street. He headed pell-mell toward the climbing toy.

"I love him, Gabe. I can't tell you how tormented I am about what happened. I can't sleep. I can't eat—"

"Shh." He put a finger to her lips. "I know. I knew all along but I let fear take control. I was wrong. Terribly, stupidly wrong. I know that now. When your brother said you were leaving town, I knew I couldn't let you go."

"You talked to Zach?"

"He gave me a call this morning. Early. Your tight-lipped brother can say more in a few well-placed words than most people can say in a lifetime."

"What did he say?"

"He said he was tired of seeing his baby sister get hurt and if I didn't have feelings for you, I should hit the road."

Brooke pressed a hand to her mouth. "Oh, Gabe, I'm sorry."

"Don't be. I like the guy. A terse man-to-man was exactly what I needed to wake up and face reality. When A.J. disappeared, all the issues with Tara came flooding back. I let past experience crowd the truth. You aren't her. You're strong and responsible and unselfish." He cupped her face.

"When I saw you stand up to Vincent, I was both proud and angry."

"I was scared to death."

"But you stood your ground. I heard what you said. You'd fight him to protect A.J. and me." He kissed her eyelid. "Do you know what that means to me?"

"What?" She offered her other eyelid. He kissed it, too. Her insides melted. The worry that he wouldn't forgive her, that she couldn't forgive herself, disappeared like hot fog.

"It means you're best thing that's happened to me in a long time. It means I can't lose you. It means if I don't tell you how much I love you, your brother's going to beat me up."

A giggle burst from Brooke's throat. She opened her eyes and tilted her head back to read his face. Oh, that beloved face. "Tell me then and mean it."

"I love you, Brooke. I loved you the minute I saw you climbing in that window and I've loved you more every day since. I realize now that's why I wanted you for A.J.'s nanny. I had to be near you. I was afraid you were too young. I was afraid I was too old, but I had to have you in my life." His lips found hers in a kiss of passion and tenderness. When the sweetness ended, he smiled softly and said, "Your turn."

"Finally," she said in mock annoyance. "Such a chatterbox. You could take lessons from my brother."

He kissed her again, this time until her head spun and her heart sang. When she came up for air, she gave her head a stunned shake. "Wow. Wow."

"Is that all you can say?"

"I love you, Gabe," she said, smiling, chest bursting with happiness. "Now, kiss me like that again."

"Glutton," he murmured, right before his lips met hers.

Epilogue

The gathering inside the fellowship hall of Clayton Christian Church was a noisy bunch. Chairs scraped, voices rose and fell, and kids played, occasionally breaking out in a game of tag.

They'd invited everyone in the church, her family and friends as well as Gabe's friends and family and employees from Denver. The invitations had simply said "a celebration," but Brooke knew Gabe had more in mind than a party. From the looks and comments Brooke received, the guests suspected the real reason for the party. Not that she cared.

She hoped Zach would come but wasn't holding her breath for tonight. He would be here soon, he'd promised, but he was still wrapping up some kind of investigation. She missed her brother, missed that strong shoulder she'd leaned on over the years. Now that she was back in Clayton for good, Brooke wanted her siblings home, too. She even had the crazy idea that she might convince Zach to take Sheriff Digger's position now that he was retiring.

Ah, well. Tonight was going to be wonderful, and having given his blessing to Gabe and her, Zach was here in her heart.

She took a long, happy breath.

Spicy barbecued pork fragranced the air. Gabe had ordered the meal, and the Hicks brothers catered the food with Arabella's able assistance. She'd baked the breads and desserts that had Brooke calculating how many miles she'd have to run this next week.

"You're killing me with those pastries," she teased as she helped line the desserts on a long, plastic-covered table.

"You can't live on love."

"Who says?"

Arabella sobered. "Speaking of which, I guess you noticed Jasmine isn't here. She's off somewhere with Cade."

"I invited both of them."

"Cade refused. Apparently, he thinks his presence would make waves." Arabella slid a knife across a pecan pie, deftly cutting the gooey sweet into eight equal pieces. "This is one of the reasons I don't want them to get married. She'll be an outcast from the family from now on."

"The feud has exacerbated since Gabe fired Vincent. I feel bad for Jasmine and Cade."

"Vincent is furious with you, that's for sure," her cousin said. "He's told everyone in town how you're out to ruin him."

"You and I know that's a lie. At least there have been no more problems at the Lucky Lady."

"For now," Arabella replied. "We also know that side of the family is not going to stop until they get their hands on Grandpa George's fortune or until someone proves they're to blame for the recent mischief."

"If Zach ever comes home, he's the perfect choice to investigate."

"If. So many ifs, Brooke." Arabella pointed a cake lifter. "Here comes your gorgeous man."

Her gorgeous man. Hers. Gabe Wesson loved her. She loved him. She could hardly believe how God had worked out a life plan once she'd gotten out of the way and given Him control.

"Can I steal my woman?"

Arabella handed Brooke a napkin. "Wipe that smirk off his face."

"I happen to love that smirk." Laughing, Brooke hooked arms with her gorgeous man and strolled away. "What's up?"

"Just wanted to be with you."

"Same here." She sighed, content. "Where's our boy?"

"Macy and her new best friend took him to the nursery to play."

"We've come a long way, haven't we?" She no longer broke out in sweat every time the boy was out of her sight. Neither did Gabe, though they both kept a careful watch. If Vincent had taken the toddler before, he might try again.

"I think we should tell Darlene about our decision tonight." Gabe nodded toward the frail woman sitting at the far end of the hall. The pastor's wife sat with her, talking.

"Tonight is perfect." They'd talked and prayed about Macy for days and both had reached the same momentous conclusion. If anything should happen to Darlene, they wanted to adopt Macy as their own. Gabe had already set up a college fund for her.

"You are such a good man. No wonder I love you madly."

"I hope you don't change your mind when I tell you what I've done."

She stepped back. "What?"

He reached into his suit jacket and took out an envelope. "A little gift."

"Gabe, you don't have to buy me things."

"What good is money if I can't spend it on the

woman I love?" He prodded her with the envelope. "You want this. You may not know you want it, but you do. Remember how I told you Emmanuel Corporation always gives back to a community?"

She removed the folded document and read. "You've started a trust fund for the Lucy Clayton Recreational Facility?"

"Only if you design and run it. I scouted out a plot of land. Perfect building site. You're already a pied piper with kids following you to the gym and the park. But if I've messed this up, if the name upsets you, if I read you wrong..."

She held the paper to her chest, sure her heart was about to burst. "Gabe. Gabe. Oh, Gabe."

"Do you approve?"

"To honor my baby sister with a living legacy is the perfect closure. The Lucy Clayton Recreational Facility is exactly what this town—and I—need." Paper crinkled against his shoulders as she threw her arms around him. Tears of happiness thickened her throat.

He held her, stroked her back, kissed her cheek and murmured sweet things. As far as Brooke was concerned she could stand here all night in Gabe's arms. This incredible man instinctively knew what she needed even when she hadn't known herself.

"Are you two going to lollygag all night or can we get this party started?" They pulled apart to see rotund Gerald Hicks eyeing them with amusement. "Folks are getting hungry. A hungry crowd is a dangerous thing."

"First a little announcement." Gabe and Brooke exchanged grins. He took her hand and drew her to the center of the room where he raised his voice. "Excuse me, everyone."

When no one heard amid the noise and chatter, Brooke raised two fingers to her lips and whistled.

At Gabe's stunned expression, she laughed. "I've been practicing."

The crowd quieted, probably as shocked as Gabe.

"We have an announcement to make."

"Figured something was up," one of his miners called. "No man springs for a spread like this without a real good reason."

A titter of laughter circled the room.

Brooke's heart danced with excitement. She knew what was coming but couldn't help bouncing a little anyway.

Taking both her hands, Gabe stood before her, strong and confident with love shining through his dark-brown eyes.

"Brooke," he said. "God has blessed my life a thousand ways. In business, with A.J., with this great little town and now with you. I don't know why He chose to bless me of all people, but He did, and I'm forever thankful. I've made my share of mistakes. I'm not perfect, not even close, but I love you. If you'll agree to be my wife, I'll do my best to be the man you need, a man you can love and be proud of. Will you marry me?"

Brooke heard Arabella's squeak and a collective gasp as air was sucked from the room. Total silence buzzed around them. If she hadn't been so moved, she'd have giggled.

Swallowing past the lump of nerves and emotion, she said, "I spent my entire adult life controlled by the past. You've helped me grow. You and A.J. and your dear, wonderful love. I can't change what happened or the heartache or the loss for either of us, but I can embrace the future and be the woman God intended me to be. I would be honored beyond words to be your wife."

As Gabe slipped the diamond solitaire engagement ring on her finger and then kissed her until her ears rang and the world faded, applause and laughter filled the fellowship hall.

The issues of the inheritance and the problems of Clayton, Colorado, still lingered on the wind unresolved, but for tonight, inside this small-town church stuffed with good friends, food and family, the issues of the heart were all that mattered.

* * * * *

Dear Reader,

There's nothing quite as creatively exciting to a writer than a new project, and when that project offers the opportunity to work with a group of talented authors, all the better. So, when my editor called with the offer to write the first book of Love Inspired's latest continuity, *Rocky Mountain Heirs*, I was happy to say yes.

I hope you've enjoyed *The Nanny's Homecoming* as much as I've enjoyed writing it for you. The wonderful Arlene James is up next with the story of Brooke's brother, Zach. You won't want to miss it!

I love hearing from readers. Please write to me through my blog at www.lindagoodnight.com or at Steeple Hill, 233 Broadway, Suite 1001, New York, NY 10279.

Until next time, peace and blessings,

Linda Goodnight

Questions for Discussion

1. What is the setting of this story? How did the setting add to or take away from the events?

2. The problems in Clayton, Colorado, began long before the book opens. Who caused the problems? What were they? How have the conflicts of the past affected the current lives of the Clayton heirs?

3. Who was your favorite character? Why? What characteristic did you find most appealing?

4. Did the characters seem real to you? Why or why not? Which were the most compelling and complex?

5. Brooke had suffered guilt over the death of her sister for many years. Do you think her reactions were realistic? Have you ever known anyone still struggling with a past trauma who simply could not "get over it"?

6. How did Gabe's deceased wife affect the relationship between him and Brooke? Was he justified in his concerns?

7. What is your opinion of age differences between a husband and wife?

8. The story contains a number of subplots, including the romance of Jasmine and Cade. Why is everyone against this couple? Do you think the families are justified in their opposition? Why or why not?

9. When Gabe's son disappears, Brooke believes Vincent is responsible. What do you think? Do you think the fact that A.J. was found in Vincent's backyard is indicative of guilt or too much of a coincidence?

10. Do you think Gabe was right to fire Vincent? What problems do you foresee happening because of this?

11. Brooke also suspects Vincent was her hooded intruder. Do you? Would her former fiancé be a more likely suspect? Why or why not?

12. Discuss Vincent Clayton's motivations. Is he in any way justified for his anger toward Brooke's family? Do he and his side of the family deserve to inherit?

13. Can you find a scripture reference concerning money? What is it? How does it apply to the

conflicts in this story? Which characters are most affected by this scripture?

14. Is it wrong for a Christian to desire wealth or to be wealthy? Find Scriptures to back up your opinion.

15. How did Brooke grow and change during the course of the story? What events served as catalysts for this growth?

16. If you could meet any of the characters in this book, who would you choose? Why?

17. Discuss the book's editing. Was it satisfying? What would you change if you could?

Love Inspired® SUSPENSE

RIVETING INSPIRATIONAL ROMANCE

Watch for our series of edge-
of-your-seat suspense novels.
These contemporary tales
of intrigue and romance
feature Christian characters
facing challenges to their faith...
and their lives!

**AVAILABLE IN REGULAR
& LARGER-PRINT FORMATS**

For exciting stories that reflect traditional values,
visit:
www.ReaderService.com